DANA MARTON

72 HOURS

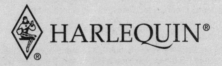
HARLEQUIN®

TORONTO • NEW YORK • LONDON
AMSTERDAM • PARIS • SYDNEY • HAMBURG
STOCKHOLM • ATHENS • TOKYO • MILAN • MADRID
PRAGUE • WARSAW • BUDAPEST • AUCKLAND

With many thanks to Allison Lyons and Denise Zaza.
And to Susan Mallery for being the wonderful friend
that she is.

ISBN-13: 978-0-373-88829-0
ISBN-10:   0-373-88829-5

72 HOURS

Touching her was a mistake.

The men hidden below them resumed talking, but he wasn't listening.

He could remember, as if it were yesterday, massaging shampoo into her hair, the two of them in the shower, water sluicing over her curves, followed by his hands. She'd been ready, had always been ready for him, and he'd lost himself in her, so much so it took his breath away.

Her low gasp brought him back to the present and he realized he had gripped her arm harder than he had meant to.

And although he couldn't see much in the dimly lit duct where they were trapped, it sure looked as if her eyes were throwing sparks. Well, as long as she was already mad at him...

He dipped his head forward and took her lips. She was soft and sweet, as mind-bending as he remembered. He had been craving this reunion from the day she had walked away, and he liked to think that now and then she had thought of him, too.

Still, it came as no surprise when she put a hand to his chest and pushed, not even whispering but breathing the words "No. Parker, no" against his mouth.

Like the bastard he was, he kissed her anyway. Because he could.

And felt immensely gratified when in the next second she melted against him.

ABOUT THE AUTHOR

Author Dana Marton lives near Wilmington, Delaware. She has been an avid reader since childhood and has a master's degree in writing popular fiction. When not writing, she can be found either in her garden or her home library. For more information on the author and her other novels, please visit her Web site at www.danamarton.com.

She would love to hear from her readers via e-mail: DanaMarton@yahoo.com

Books by Dana Marton

HARLEQUIN INTRIGUE
 902—ROGUE SOLDIER
 917—PROTECTIVE MEASURES
 933—BRIDAL OP
 962—UNDERCOVER SHEIK
 985—SECRET CONTRACT*
 991—IRONCLAD COVER*
1007—MY BODYGUARD*
1013—INTIMATE DETAILS*
1039—SHEIK SEDUCTION
1055—72 HOURS

*Mission: Redemption

CAST OF CHARACTERS

Parker McCall—This undercover soldier knows how to disarm a nuclear warhead, but when faced with the only woman he ever loved, will he be able to save her as well as the other hostages whose lives depend on him?

Kate Hamilton—Her life is in grave danger when her ex-fiancé charges to the rescue. Through their mad escape, she begins to realize that she never really knew the man. And the new Parker might be more than she can resist.

Piotr Morovich—A known anarchist and mercenary. Is it possible that he's working for the Tarkmez rebels this time?

Victor Sergeyevich—Former KBG agent who is responsible for the death of Piotr's father.

Ivan—A Russian embassy guard. Is he there to protect the embassy staff, or does he have another agenda?

Colonel Wilson—Head of the Special Designation Defense Unit.

SDDU—Special Designation Defense Unit, a top secret military team established to fight terrorism. Its existence is known by only a select few. Members are recruited from the best of the best.

Chapter One

A good spy had many tools at his disposal. One of them was the instinctual knowledge of when to run. Parker McCall was running for his life, toward the Tuileries on Rue de Rivoli that stretched parallel to the River Seine.

When he'd been on jungle missions, running for the river was a good idea most of the time, and often the only way out. But right now he was on a street dense with tourists. Jumping into the Seine would do nothing but draw attention to himself and bring the authorities.

He hated Paris. It was the city that had taken Kate away from him.

"Excusez-moi." He slipped between two businessmen deep in discussion, blocking the sidewalk.

The chase scenes they showed in action movies, where seasoned professionals madly scrambled from their pursuers, knocking over vendor stands and causing all kinds of commotion, were nonsense. When you were hunted, you went to ground. You went quietly, did everything you could to blend in and become invisible, part of the usual tapestry of local life. You ran in such a way that nobody looking at you could tell you were running.

He glanced at his watch again, deepened the annoyed scowl on his face and smoothed down his tie as he moved briskly through the crowd. He was a businessman late for a dinner. And the throng of people who'd seen hundreds of late businessmen rushing through identified him as such and parted in front of him, paying him scant attention. He was swimming through people and he had to be careful not to cause any ripples. Ripples would be noticed.

And his enemies were watching.

He figured at least four men were after him. He had caught glimpses, but mostly he operated by instinct.

They, too, were professionals. Professional killers who moved through the city the way the lions of Africa moved forward in the cover of the tall grass, in a well-coordinated hunt, invisible until they were but a jump away from their prey.

"Excusez-moi." He stepped around a twin stroller and glanced up at the large *M* sign a few yards ahead—Le Métro, Paris's famed subway system. He could try to disappear there or go for the Tuileries and see if he could deal with the men in the garden.

The subway would be packed. This was one of the busiest stations, the one closest to the Musée du Louvre. He could get away without confrontation.

But he wanted more. Information was the name of the game. And right now, the information he needed was the identity of the man who had sicced his henchmen on Parker. He had too many enemies to take a blind guess.

Like New York, Paris never slept. Especially not on hot summer evenings. Tourists and locals filled the streets.

He moved forward and could see the garden at last. He crossed the Avenue du Général Lemonnier and hurried to the nearest entrance. The sixty-three acres of mostly open landscaping that lay before him was enough to make anyone stop in wonder, but he didn't have the time to enjoy the sight. He planned and calculated.

The lions that hunted him were hidden in the tall grass. At least he didn't have to worry about the approaching darkness and not being able to see. They didn't call Paris the city of light—in addition to love—for nothing. It was lit up like Methuselah's birthday cake.

Head for higher ground. Get a good vantage point. But there weren't many of those in the garden, so he strode toward the Ferris wheel.

Too late.

A blur of movement caught his attention by the pedestal of a large statue. They'd gotten in front of him. Or at least one of them had. But hunters as good as these four didn't reveal themselves by accident. Parker had a feeling that he'd been supposed to see that. They wanted him to run in the opposite direction. They were trying to herd him someplace out of sight where they could take him out.

He strode to the statues instead, feinted in one direction and went around the other. He didn't take the time to look or evaluate. His fist connected with a man's face in the next second. He caught the guy as he staggered back, then looped the man's arm around his shoulder, holding his gun against his side, and dragged him off into the stand of trees nearby, away from the curious gazes of passersby. Nobody would be walking off the paved paths today. The ground was muddy from this morning's rain.

"Who are you?" He was disarming the man as he spoke, confiscating first his gun, then the near-microscopic communications device attached to the guy's ear. "Who sent you here?"

The man—in his mid-thirties, around six feet, cropped hair—had a swarthy skin tone and that wide Slavic facial type that marked him from somewhere around the Black Sea. He pressed his thin lips together and went for the knife that had been hidden up his sleeve. Parker turned the blade and drove it home. No time for a tussle, to subdue him then get him to talk, although he could have made him talk, given some time. But the others could be here any second.

He lowered the body to the ground and searched the man's clothes, found no identification. He hadn't expected any.

One down, three to go. He headed out of the woods.

He'd come to Paris on the trail of Piotr Morovich, a slippery Russian mercenary who'd been discovered to have connections to a Middle Eastern terrorist group his team had been watching. But he'd run into something bigger than he had anticipated. Good thing that handling the unexpected was his specialty.

He moved through the strolling tourists and children playing and reached the Ferris wheel. His tie was off now, his jacket swung over his shoulder, his body language the same as all the other casual sightseers'.

"One ticket, *s'il vous plaît.*" He scanned the tourists already on the ride. *"Merci,"* he said, then boarded the Ferris wheel.

The giant wheel turned slowly, taking him higher and higher. But while the others oohed and aahed over the sights, he was watching the people below.

There. One of the men he was looking for was coming down the central walkway. Parker looked even more carefully and spotted another by the fountain. Where was the third? Where would *he* be in the same situation? Every hunt had a pattern; he just had to find it.

He watched the two men as they looked for him and for their lost teammate who wasn't checking in over the radio. The four would have formed a U originally, trying to get him in the middle. He looked in the direction of the river. And he found the third man.

He was impatient now for his cart to reach the ground again, keeping his eyes on the men. He would get them one by one, would get some answers.

His phone buzzed in his pocket. He pulled it out and glanced at the display, intending to return the call later. Then he saw the coded ID flashing on the small screen—the Colonel.

"Sir?"

"This evening at 21:03 hours, Tarkmez rebel forces overtook the Russian Embassy on Rue de Prony," the head of the SDDU, Secret Designation Defense Unit, one of the U.S.'s most effective covert weapons against terrorism, said.

The hundred-plus-member unit did everything from reconnaissance to demolition, personnel extraction, spying, kidnapping and assassinations. Parker himself had done it all. He glanced at his watch—21:25.

"The Russians haven't made it public yet. They haven't even notified the French authorities," the Colonel went on.

He didn't have to ask how the CIA, from whom the Colonel had no doubt gotten his information, would know this fast. They'd had the Russian embassy bugged for decades. Well, on and off. The Russians were as efficient at sweeping out the bugs as the agency was creative at placing them.

"The U.S. consul was at an unscheduled, informal dinner with the Russian ambassador and his wife. She is in the building, but we don't have an exact location on her."

While ambassadors represented the head of their country and there was only one of them, consuls handled visa applications and all the various problems of U.S. citizens abroad, representing their country in general, the position more administrative than political. The U.S. had about a dozen consuls in France.

But Parker had a bad premonition, cold dread settling into his stomach. "Kate?"

"Affirmative."

The single word slammed into his chest with the force of a .22 bullet.

"Is she okay?" Tightly locked away emotions broke free, one after the other, tripping his heartbeat.

"We don't know. The Russians are not good at asking for help. It's possible that they'll keep the situation secret for several hours, unless the rebels themselves make contact with the media."

His cart was approaching the ground. Ten feet, nine, eight, close enough. There were times for blending in, then there were times to break all the rules, even if it did draw attention. He lifted the safety bar and stood, eliciting a warning cry from the operator and loud comments and gasps from bystanders. He jumped and landed in a crouch, staying down so the next seat wouldn't knock him over the head, then sprinted into the crowd.

"What do the rebels want?" he asked, scanning the park for the men. His business with them would have to wait.

"Don't know yet. Probably autonomy. We can't offer help to the Russians until they tell us about the problem. Saying anything now would be tantamount to admitting that we have their embassy bugged. Considering the current political climate, the last thing we need is to cause an international incident," the Colonel said. "Be careful. This has all the makings of a disaster."

Pictures of news reports flashed through Parker's mind: the infamous Dubrovka theater siege and the Ossetia school-hostage

crises. The Russian elite Alpha counterterrorism troops and their Vymple special forces,
like their U.S. counterparts, were known for
not negotiating with terrorists. Unfortunately, they were also known for getting their
enemies at any price, even at the cost of
innocent lives. In the theater siege, 115
hostages were killed, in the school standoff,
over 300, many of them children.

Parker popped his earpiece into place,
tucked away his phone and broke into a flat
run. The men who hunted him would have to
wait. The embassy had been taken only
minutes ago. There was a small chance that
the entire behemoth of a building hadn't
been secured yet by the rebels. The sooner
he got there, the better his chances were for
getting in.

"Of the few men we have in the area, you're
the closest," the Colonel said. "And you know
the most about the Tarkmezi situation."

And Parker suspected that the Colonel had
also taken his private connection into consid-
eration, knew he would want to be involved.
Not that the Colonel would ever admit to
personal favors.

"I appreciate it, sir," he told the man anyway.
Rain began to fall again.

"Do try to remember that this is a minimum-impact, covert mission," the Colonel said in a meaningful tone.

Which meant that he was to make as little contact as possible, remain close to invisible as he searched for Kate and got her out. He was to change nothing, interact with no other aspects of the situation but those strictly required for the extraction.

"And the other hostages?"

"As soon as their country asks for our help we'll give it. Our hands are tied until then."

That idea didn't sit too well with him. He hated when politics interfered with a mission of his, which happened about every damned time.

"Parker?" The Colonel's tone changed to warning. "Don't make me regret that I tagged you for this job."

"No, sir."

"Just get Kate Hamilton out."

"Yes, sir."

That he would. Yeah, he was still mad at Kate for leaving him. Mad as hell, but he wasn't going to let any harm come to her. Any Tarkmez rebel bastard who laid a hand on the woman he'd once meant to marry was going to answer to him.

August 9, 23:45

"Do you have visual?" The question came through his cell phone. His battery was at twenty-five percent so Parker was rationing his calls to the Colonel. But he had called in to report that he was inside.

He tapped the phone once in response. He was trying to speak as little as possible, wasn't sure who could overhear him as he docked in the vent system that had openings to the various rooms. One tap meant no, two taps yes.

At least four of the gunmen who had overtaken the building were talking in the room below him. He could hear no one else. If there were hostages in there, they were kept quiet.

"I'm scrambling to get you some backup, but I can't pull anyone who's near enough," the Colonel said.

He understood. His team was specifically created for undercover missions. A lot of the members were built into terrorist organizations, rebel groups around the world or sleeper cells. To pull one at a moment's notice before his or her job was done would ruin months or years of undercover work.

"I'm going to get someone else in to help as fast as I can," the Colonel went on.

Parker tapped *no*. He'd snuck in before the embassy had been fully secured. Anyone trying to get in now would have to fight their way in. And that could mean disaster for the hostages. He could bring Kate out on his own.

Muted pops came from somewhere behind him. He immediately reversed direction.

"Gunshots. Two," he whispered into the phone.

"I'll check it out. Contact me if there's anything else," the Colonel said and then he was gone.

Those bugs hidden throughout the embassy were still transmitting. From his CIA connection, the Colonel should be able to get some information on what was happening. Parker backed through the vent duct as fast as he could. Since the weather was cool and overcast, the air-conditioning wasn't on; there was nothing to hide the noise he made. So he didn't make any.

He had a rough idea of the building's outline. The Colonel had briefed him on the way over. Since Kate had last been heard near the kitchens, he'd been heading in that direction, surveying all the rooms he could see as he went. So far he'd seen or heard a dozen or so rebels but no hostages.

The gunshots changed everything. There was a better-than-fair chance that the hostages were that way. His phone vibrated. He opened it without halting his progress.

"Bad news." The Colonel's grim tone underscored his words. "To prove how serious they are, the rebels just shot Ambassador Vasilievits."

Parker went faster, crawling with grim determination, one hundred percent focused on the job. Kate had been with the ambassador and his wife at the time of the initial attack on the embassy. He hoped she had somehow been separated from them and had managed to escape the rebels' notice.

Because if she hadn't, if the rebels figured out who Kate was, she would be next. They hated Americans as much as they hated the Russians.

He wished he had prepared for more than surveillance before he'd left his hotel late that afternoon and then run into the four men who'd seemed hell-bent on taking him out. He had nothing but his gun and his cell phone with its dwindling battery. Right now he would have given anything for the full tool kit that waited hidden behind the ceiling tiles of his hotel room.

"Any publicity on this yet?" he asked, able to talk more freely having gotten into a section that didn't have any openings to rooms.

"Nothing. The Russians might not break silence until morning. Their counterterrorism team is on its way. We don't think they asked the French for permission, but once the team is in place there isn't much the French can do. That's all I have."

They ended the connection, and he kept crawling. When he reached the next vertical drop, he lowered himself inch by inch, stopping when he heard voices ahead. The men were talking in Tarkmezi.

"And if they gas us?" The speaker sounded on edge.

"That's what we have the masks for," came the calm reply.

"What if they have something new and nasty? Kill us before we get the masks on."

"Get it on and keep it on, then," another guy snapped. "Maybe it'll shut you up."

"What do you think's going on?" The worrywart on the team didn't seem to be able to stop himself. "I wonder if they are negotiating?"

"When there's something to know, Piotr will tell us."

Parker picked his head up at the mention of the name. What were the chances that this was his Piotr? It was a common name, the Russian equivalent of Peter. But his instincts prickled. Could be that this was why Piotr Morovich had come to Paris. And if that was the case, then he hadn't come alone, something that U.S. intelligence had failed to detect.

"I could go check," Worrywart said.

"You stay the hell here."

The men fell silent just as Parker reached the vent hole.

Three Tarkmezi fighters, armed to the teeth, stood among two dozen tied-up hostages who were sitting in the middle of the floor in some sort of a gym, probably set up for embassy staff. He zeroed in on Kate and his heart rate sped up.

Hello, Kate. How have you been? He'd pictured, on too many occasions, the two of them meeting up again after all this time, but he had never imagined it would be under these circumstances.

She looked unharmed and calm. The spring that had been wound tightly in his chest since the Colonel had called now eased.

Her hair was different from when he'd last seen her—a classy, sexy bob. He felt a ping of annoyance. Why had she changed? For whom? He had loved to run his fingers through her long, honey-blond hair. She had lost weight, too, but not much, still had those curves that used to drive him mad.

Memories flashed into his mind—hot, sweaty and explicit—and his body tightened. For a second he was transported back to the past, with Kate under him, her back bowed, her silky hair fanned out on the pillow, that soft moan of hers escaping her full lips as she looked at him the way she had always looked at him during their intense lovemaking, straight in the eyes. Man, it used to turn him on.

Not much had changed since, he realized ruefully and shifted in the tight space.

Keeping control with her in bed had always been a challenge. One of the many things he had loved about her. A single touch and all he could think was fast and hard, now, now, now. Slow and easy took superhuman effort. Pleasurable, highly gratifying effort. He pushed that thought as far away as he could. He couldn't go back there now. Not now, not ever.

One of the rebels moved and blocked her from view.

Come on, get out of the way. Parker gritted his teeth until the man finally moved again.

Kate stretched her long legs without getting up. In her dark slacks, white top and a cook's jacket, she blended in with the other half dozen kitchen staff among the hostages. Where were the rest? He didn't see any of the security team that would have guarded the embassy.

He focused on the three rebels. They would have to be distracted and neutralized before he could go in to save Kate. He surveyed the room, noting every detail, including the position of the doors and windows and their distance from each other, every piece of exercise equipment that could be used as a weapon or for cover. He swore silently at the floor-to-ceiling mirrors that lined the walls and made it impossible to sneak up behind anyone.

The easiest thing would be to go in predawn when the guards were ready to nod off, exhausted by their night vigil. But he hated the thought of waiting that long. He wanted her out before the Russian counter-terrorism team got here.

He preferred planned and coordinated operations where nothing was left to chance. But those took time. And Kate's life was at stake. To save her he would do anything.

"Hang in there." He mouthed the words as he pulled his gun and screwed on the silencer, preparing to make his move.

The Colonel had asked him not to leave any signs—meaning a string of dead bodies—that he'd been there, if he could help it. Well, looked like he couldn't.

August 10, 00:05

SHE HAD Parker on her mind and that annoyed her no end. Kate Hamilton stared at the floor, not daring to make eye contact with the rebels.

They left the hostages alone for the most, but gave orders now and then that they expected to be followed, a problem since Kate didn't speak Russian. All the embassy staff did, even the French employees; it was a condition of employment here, just as fluent knowledge of English was a condition of employment over at the U.S. embassy. She was smart enough to copy whatever the others did in response to the commands. It had worked so far, but she wasn't sure how long her luck would hold out.

"Try something," Anna, a slightly built, petite young woman whispered barely audibly to her left. She was French and the personal secretary to the ambassador's wife.

Try something. Brilliant idea. Except that her hands were bound and three nasty-looking AK-47s were pointed in her general direction.

Parker would know what to do. He spoke a dozen languages. And he could always handle tough situations. The way he'd handled an attempted mugging when they'd gone down to Florida for a long weekend came to mind. She supposed he'd had to learn. He visited dangerous parts of the world as a foreign correspondent for Reuters. His continued absence had driven her nuts during their engagement.

She refused to let the memories hurt anymore. She was better off without him.

She pressed her lips together and looked around the room for the hundredth time, trying to figure out a way she could make a break for it and not be shot within a fraction of a second. *Okay, Parker. What would you do?* The gunshots they had heard earlier didn't fill her with optimism.

Several embassy guards had been killed within the first few minutes of the attack, as well as the sole civilian-dressed bodyguard who had escorted her over from the U.S. embassy for an unofficial visit with Tanya, the Russian ambassador's wife.

Tanya had left the dinner table for just a moment to take her two young girls to their nanny when the rebels had rushed in. Maybe they'd been able to escape. The rebels had taken her husband, the ambassador, immediately and herded the rest of the people in here, along with other staff they'd found around the embassy that late in the evening.

It was Anna who had begged the white coat off a cook's assistant and given it to Kate, warning her not to speak English, not to reveal who she was. And Kate had kept quiet, although she wasn't sure if it was the right thing to do. Being a U.S. consul came with a certain amount of respect for the title and the full backing of the American government. Maybe if she'd spoken up, the rebels would have decided they didn't want to tangle with the U.S. and would have let her go. She shifted on the hard floor. Maybe she should tell them now.

Or maybe not. She still wasn't over the shock of seeing the bullet rip through her bodyguard's head. She swallowed and squeezed her eyes shut, trying not to think of Jeff as he'd lain there on the dining room floor in a pool of his own blood. He and the sole Russian guard who'd been inside the dining room were badly outnumbered when the rebels had poured in.

"Pochemu tu…" One of the armed men launched into a tirade.

She wished she could understand what he was talking about, what they were discussing. The lanky one seemed to be whining a lot. The oldest of the three ignored him for the most part. The short, pudgy one kept snapping at him, then finally gave up and shrugged with a disgusted groan.

The whiner swung his rifle over his shoulder and walked out the door, letting it slam behind him.

"Two," Anna whispered.

They were down to two guards. This could be the best chance they were going to get to try something—disarm them, maybe, and get to the phone on the wall by the gym's door, call for help. Breaking out of the embassy didn't seem possible. Too many armed rebels secured the building.

She tried to establish eye contact with the chef who appeared to be in good shape, then with two other guys, tall, beefy and Slavic-looking with hard features and dirty-blond hair. They looked alike, possibly related.

They seemed to be the largest and strongest men in the room.

Come on. Over here. She fidgeted and managed to get the attention of one of them. She wiggled her eyebrows toward the guards. The guy looked back nonplussed.

Since her hands were tied behind her back, she couldn't make any hand signals. She kept wiggling her eyebrows and nodding with her head. The guy smiled.

Probably thought she was coming on to him. Did she look like a complete idiot? Apparently so, because he wiggled his eyebrows back.

She stifled a groan and rolled her eyes in a *never-mind* look she hoped translated. And felt a hand on hers.

She turned slowly toward the other side and met Anna's gaze. The woman glanced toward the guards then back at Kate with a questioning look in her large blue eyes. Kate nodded. *Yes, yes, that's what I've been trying to do.*

"Now," Anna breathed without moving her lips. She took a deep breath then started to cry.

The pudgy guard yelled at her immediately. Anna stifled her sobs and leaned against Kate as if for support. She tugged on the nylon cuffs that held Kate's hands behind her back.

Then came heat. Under the noise of her crying, apparently she had lit a match or a lighter that must have been hidden in her pocket.

Every snarly thought Kate had ever had about smokers blowing smoke in her face at the cafés that supported her French-pastry habit, she took back.

Ouch. Even a small flame could be pretty hot this close. But the pressure of the nylon eased on her wrists, and in the next second she was free.

"Hurry," the girl whispered into her shoulder and dropped a lighter into her hands.

But then the door opened and the whiny guard was back, carrying a large box, leading with his back. Or maybe it wasn't the whiny guard. This one looked bigger. But familiar.

The pudgy rebel barked a question.

"Da, da." The newcomer mumbled the rest of his answer and kept advancing into the room, groaning, bent under the weight of whatever he was carrying. But the next second the box flew at the older bandit, knocking his weapon aside while the stranger took out the pudgy one with his gun. He had enough time to shoot the other one, too, before that one gathered himself.

Her hands were free, but all she could do was stare at the man dumbstruck, unable to believe her eyes.

Parker?

She pushed to her feet and stepped toward him, but he shook his head slightly and severed eye contact as if he didn't want anyone to know that they knew each other. He spoke in Russian as he cut the plastic cuffs off people then distributed the rebels' guns to the hostages, who were asking questions at the rate of a hundred per second.

He answered before he pointed at her, said something else in Russian and ripped the gas mask off Pudgy's belt, then shoved it into her hand. He dragged her out of the gym, closing the door behind them.

"What's going on?" She followed him down the corridor since he wouldn't stop. "What are you involved with now?" He looked even better than he had in her frequent dreams of him. Whoever she'd been with in the two years since they'd broken up, her dreams brought only one man to her: Parker.

He couldn't be here on assignment. That wouldn't make any sense. "If the press could get in, why isn't the rescue team here?"

"Later." His whole body alert, the gun

poised to shoot, he moved so fast that keeping up was an effort. He looked like Parker's action-figure twin: eyes hard as flint, body language tight and on the scary side. Even his voice sounded sharper.

She'd never seen him like this before. Pictures of the last few minutes flashed into her head, the way he had shot those men. He sure hadn't looked like a reporter back there. She struggled to make sense of it all. Then, as they rushed forward, her gaze snagged on a security camera high up on the wall—not pointing at the row of antique oil paintings but at the hallway itself.

"Can they see us?" She looked around, bewildered, expecting to run into rebel soldiers any second.

"They're not working. The rebels took out the security system when they broke in. Phones are disabled, too. I already checked."

Where? How? She didn't have time to ask.

Voices came from up ahead. *No, no, no.* A fresh wave of panic hit just when she thought she was already at max capacity for fear. They were in a long, marble-tiled hallway with a single, ornately gilded door they'd just passed.

Parker pulled back immediately and

reached for the knob. Locked. He looked around, searching the corridor.

Why didn't he just kick the door in? She was about to ask when she realized they couldn't afford to make noise. Good thing one of them had a clear enough mind to think.

The voices neared. Parker let go of her and hurried to an ornamental cast-iron grid low on the opposite wall, pulled a nasty-looking knife and began to unscrew it.

They were never going to make it. She looked back and forth between him and the end of the hallway. *Hurry, hurry, hurry.* "They're almost here."

He got the heavy-looking grid off and laid it down gently, without making a sound. Then he climbed in, legs first. She was practically on top of him. But he didn't move lower to make room for her. "Get on my back," he said.

"What? I can't. It's—" She didn't have time to argue. The rebels were coming.

She went in, legs first like he did, feeling awkward and uncomfortable at having to touch him, having to hang on to him, being pressed against his wide back. He was all hard muscle just as he'd always been. She snipped any stray memory in the bud and kept moving. When she had her arms around his neck and her legs around his waist as if he were giving her a piggyback ride, she stopped, barely daring to breathe. She wasn't crazy about dark, tight places.

And they weren't in some storage nook as she had thought, but in a vertical, chimneylike tunnel with a bottomless drop below them.

But just when she thought things couldn't get more dangerous, he let go with his left hand and reached for the cast-iron grid to lift it back into place. Boots passed in front of their hiding place a few seconds later, people talking.

The men stopped to chat just out of sight. *Oh God, please just go.*

They didn't. They stayed and stayed and stayed. Her arms were aching from the effort. She could barely hold herself. She couldn't see how Parker was able to hold the weight of two bodies with nothing but his fingers.

An eternity passed. Then another. She distracted herself by organizing her half-million questions about his sudden appearance and his complete personality change.

"Hang on," he whispered under his breath and moved beneath her.

She barely breathed her response. "I think

we should stay still." No need to take any unnecessary chances, make some noise and
draw attention.

"Can't. We're slipping."

All her questions cleared in the blink of an
eye, replaced by a single thought. They were
going to die.

Chapter Two

Kate braced a hand against the wall and realized at once why they were slipping. The brick was covered with slippery powder. She could make out some cobwebs in what little light filtered through the metal grid. She didn't want to think of the number of spiders that would be living in a place like this. She put the hand back around Parker's neck.

He slipped another inch.

Oh God, oh God, oh God. Please, please, please. She held her breath, expecting a fall any second. How high were they? And what was waiting for them at the bottom? Too dark to tell.

"Parker?"

"Relax," he whispered; he could probably feel the tension in her body.

She loosened the death grip she had

around his neck. Whatever he was doing to save them, he could probably do it better if she didn't cut off his air supply.

He was slipping even though he had both hands and feet braced on the side walls. But they had a slow, controlled descent; he was able to achieve at least that much. After the first few moments of sheer panic, she unfolded her legs from around his waist and stuck them out, hoping to take some of her weight off him and help to slow them even more. The less they slipped, the shorter their climb would be back to the opening once the rebels moved away.

She succeeded, but only marginally. They were still steadily going down.

At least they weren't crashing. She concentrated on the spot of light that was getting closer and closer, coming from the next cover grid on the floor below them. An eternity passed before they reached it.

Hanging on to the cast-iron scrolls, Parker was able to halt their downward progress temporarily.

They listened, but could hear no voices from outside.

"Can we get out?" she whispered.

"Maybe." He waited a beat. "Looks

deserted out there. We still have to be careful. I'm sure they secured every floor."

"They can't have people in every hallway." At least, she really hoped they couldn't.

"They don't. They're set up in strategic control positions." Parker pushed against the grid, his muscles flexing against her.

The metal didn't budge.

"Want me to get your knife out of your pocket?" she offered, although his pocket was the last place she wanted to be moseying around.

"Screws are on the outside. Can't get to them." He made another attempt at rattling them loose without success. "The offer is tempting, but I'll pass for now."

She bit back a retort at his teasing. She could and would let things go. She had learned over the years. "What do we do now?"

"Get to the bottom and find another way up." He didn't seem too shaken by their situation.

She, on the other hand, was going nuts in the confines of the tight space. "What is this place?" Her muscles tensed further as they began sliding again.

"The building used to belong to some nobleman back in the day. This is where the servants pulled up the buckets of coal from the basement for the tile stoves that heated his parlors."

"And you know this how?"

He couldn't shrug in their precarious situation, but made some small movement that gave the same effect.

Their shoes scraped on the walls that were less than three feet from each other, but the old coal dust muted the sound. She let go with one hand again and tried to find support. Carrying their combined weight had to be difficult even for a man as strong as Parker.

"I think I can do this on my own." She'd seen rock-climbing done at the gym before, how those climbers supported their weight with nothing but the tips of their fingers and toes.

"We came from the second floor. With the twenty-foot ceilings these old palaces have, the drop to the basement could be fifty feet or more," he said. "You stay where you are. If you slip, you die."

She was perfectly clear on the hundred and one ways she could die in their given situation. She was trying hard not to think of them, thank you very much. "What can I do to make this easier?"

"Stop moving."

She stilled and kept silent for a while before she realized she could probably move her lips.

"How did you get in here? Don't tell me it's for a story."

"I quit that job. I work for the government now."

He always had been dark and mysterious, something that had drawn her to him at the beginning of their relationship but had ended up driving a wedge between them eventually. Mysterious was fine in a sexy stranger. But when you were trying to build a life with someone, there were things you needed to know. There had come a time when she had realized that he was never going to let her in fully.

"You're a marine?" The U.S. embassy was protected by marines. She had expected them to come after her eventually. But Parker wasn't part of that team. He was probably too old for enlistment at this stage. She thought the age limit was twenty-eight. He was four years older than her, which made him thirty-six.

"Something like that," he said, and in typical Parker fashion, wouldn't elaborate.

She had a few guesses as to why. So her

ex was some kind of special commando. "Something like" a marine. A picture was beginning to take shape in her mind. "Did you know I was here?"

She made sure to hold her elbows in, and her knees, although that wasn't an easy task since her legs were wrapped around his waist for support. She couldn't hold herself up by her arms alone any longer. On second thought, her brilliant idea of going down on her own might have been overly optimistic.

She tried hard not to think of the countless times her legs had been wrapped around his waist from the other side. Slow breath in. Slow breath out. The stifling air of the stupid coal chute seemed unbearably hot.

"I've been briefed," he was saying.

He? What about the rest of the commando team? And in that moment, she knew without a doubt that there were no others. The embassy wasn't being liberated. She was. Through some crazy plan, he was here to rescue her, and they were about to leave all those other people behind.

As if she would ever agree to anything as insane as that.

They were just reaching the landing, had to get down on their hands and knees to crawl out, touching each other way more in the process than she was comfortable with. He had always had an instant, mind-melting effect on her. There should be a vaccination against men like him, something that would give the recipient immunity. She'd be first in line at the clinic.

A dim security light burned somewhere, enough to see that they were both black, covered in hundred-year-old soot. He looked like some Greek hero, sculpted from black marble instead of white. She glanced down at her own clothes, stifling a sigh. She looked like an Old West horse thief, tarred and waiting to be feathered.

"Come on, we don't have much time." He moved forward, gun in hand. "I came in through the roof, but we'll see if there's a way out through here. Maybe some connection to the neighboring building. Like a secret emergency tunnel for the embassy staff."

She thought of Anna, who had risked her life to melt the cuffs off her, and the kitchen staff who'd risked their lives to conceal her identity. She thought of Tanya and the two small children, and Ambassador Vasilievits, who had been separated from the others by the rebels.

"Did anyone make it out of the building?"

"No," Parker said without turning around.

He was a dozen feet ahead before he realized that she wasn't following and turned around. "What's going on?" His eyes flashed with impatience.

She had a feeling he was about to get even more unhappy with her. "I'm not leaving," she said.

WHAT in hell?

"You're leaving, babe, believe me. You're leaving if I have to carry you." His blood pressure was inching up. For some unfathomable reason, she didn't comprehend that every second counted. Odd really, because Kate Hamilton was one sharp woman.

"I'm not leaving the rest of the hostages to die. As soon as someone goes into the gym and realizes what you did, they'll be massacred." She was shooting him an accusing look, standing tall like some movie heroine.

Oh, man. She had that stubborn determination in her fine eyes, the same rich green color as the highland forests of Scotland. And he knew from experience that meant nothing good.

"I left them armed."

No way was he going to stop to have a fight about this with her. He scanned the basement instead, which seemed closed to the outside, the only exit being a staircase that led up to the ground floor. He could see a few spots on the brick walls where at one point in the past there had been basement windows to the street, but they were walled in. And since the building was an old one, the outer walls were close to three feet wide, solid brick and mortar. They couldn't even dig their way out.

"They are admin staff and people from the kitchen." Kate wouldn't let the subject drop. Her full and delicately shaped lips were set in a strict line of displeasure.

"The rebels won't kill them. They need someone to negotiate with." He eyed the stairs and calculated.

"They can negotiate with the ambassador," she countered, backing away from him as he began stalking her. "The rebels have him someplace else in the embassy. He was taken away from the rest of us at the beginning."

He stilled.

"Parker? What happened to him?"

And when he didn't respond, she asked with horror in her eyes, "They killed him? That's what the gunfire was about, wasn't it?"

He said nothing.

Her tanned hands flew up to cover the lower part of her face until only her big, luminous eyes showed, glinting with moisture. Her shoulders drooped with defeat.

"Tanya…" Her voice sounded as if she was fighting for air. "How about his wife and the—" She didn't seem to be able to take in enough air to finish the sentence.

"No idea." He felt remorseful, but undeterred. "We are leaving. Now."

"No. It's *my* life."

And his breath caught, because that had been the last thing she had told him before she'd left. *It's my life, Parker. I'm sorry. I have to do what's best.* And he had stood there, without a word, without trying to change her mind, and watched her walk away.

Letting her go had been the single most selfless thing he had ever done in his life. He knew she was better off without him. He was darkness and she was light.

But it had still hurt like hell.

He blinked hard, waited for the tightness in his chest to ease. "What are you doing here, anyway?"

"None of your business," she snapped at him. "I'm not going. I'm serious."

So was he.

"Kate." The word came out in a low growl of temper. He hated how quickly she could make him lose his cool. He was frustrated that she wouldn't give him her full cooperation.

She hesitated another long second. Damn. There had been a time when she had told him everything, had laid her soul bare and shared it. Well, the trust was gone now. He should have expected that.

"I am considering adopting a child from Russia. Tanya has two adopted children. I had some questions about the process and the orphanage she used," she said with a defensive set of her chin and a hint of vulnerability around her.

That wasn't the answer he had expected. The words cut him off at the knees. There had been a time when he was looking forward to Kate having *his* children, although he had tried to tell her that the time wasn't right just yet, that they would probably have to wait a couple of years. He didn't want to miss anything. He didn't want to be an absentee father on active duty. Not that he'd been able to tell her that. He'd had to cook up some stupid story about how he needed a lot of time at that point because he was fighting hard for his next promotion.

A tidal wave of regrets slammed into him. He couldn't think about all that now. He had to get her out of here.

But she wasn't done fighting yet. "Listen to me. Chances are they would have let the hostages go at the end. Now that you shot their men, they are going to kill the people we left behind. *Because of me.* I can't live with that. I'm not that kind of person. I can't." There was urgency and desperation in her voice. "Please," she added with her unique mix of vulnerability and determination.

She wasn't a delicate woman. She was vivacious. She had lively eyes, a full mouth and a stubborn jawline. She laughed from the heart and cried from the heart.

He still had a crush on her. The realization caught him off guard. That rush of attraction, the magnetic pull. A crush—that was all it was. He imagined there wasn't a man who could go within ten feet of Kate Hamilton without developing a little crush on her.

He could disarm a nuclear warhead. He should be able to neutralize some leftover attraction.

"Parker?"

She wouldn't give up. She wasn't the type. When someone needed help, Kate Hamilton was your gal. She'd charged to the rescue of neighbors, friends and coworkers alike, making time to find homes for strays she picked up on the street. Which made her a fine consul, he supposed, since part of her job was to assist U.S. citizens who ran into trouble here in France. She could manage a problem like nobody's business.

"Please?"

Those eyes were going to be the death of him. Oh, hell, when had he ever been able to resist her?

He drew a deep breath, recognizing himself for the fool he was. "Okay. I'll get you out. Once you're safe, I'll come back to see what I can do for the others." And the Colonel was probably going to fry his ass. A freaking barbecue.

"How can you even think about taking only me?" She was outraged and not bothering to hide it.

"Because that is precisely the order I got." He kept his voice deceptively low, although his blood was fairly boiling.

"From whom?"

He stayed silent.

"Some orders need to be questioned."

She'd never met the Colonel. "Maybe you question too much," he said.

"We should go back for them right now." Her voice had a lot of steel in it.

Something told him Kate had toughened up a lot since he'd last seen her. Or maybe that core of steel had been there all along, and he'd just never seen it because he'd been too busy running from one mission to the next, never having enough time for her, always leaving her behind.

No wonder she had walked out.

He watched her in the dim light and fought against the tide of emotions. *No regrets.* Not now. He walled off the memories. They could reminisce once they got out of this hellhole.

But first he had to placate her and gain her cooperation. Her cooperation! He was here to save her, dammit. She was supposed to jump into his arms, misty with gratitude. If he'd had more time, he would have spent a moment or two enjoying that fantasy.

"How about this? I'll neutralize as many rebels on our way out as I can, evening the odds for the hostages whom we are *temporarily* leaving behind." Even though a silent exit would have been by far preferable and had been specifically requested by the Colonel. "I'll do whatever I can for the hostages on our way out as long as it doesn't put you in jeopardy. That's non-negotiable."

She looked around thoughtfully, as if taking stock of the basement, then back at him. "We bring the hostages down here. They can barricade themselves until help comes. There's only one entrance to the basement. The rebels might not even find them down here by the time the building is taken back. Nobody gets killed because of me. That's non-negotiable."

She was managing the problem.

She was insane. And yet, the plan did have some merit. And damn, but he liked her pluck. Always had. He'd always liked everything about her.

All they had to do was go back up to the second floor where the gym was and make sure the hostages got to the coal chute without being seen. The hostages would come down, Kate and he would go up the two extra floors to the roof. They had to pass through the second floor anyway. Once they were at the gym, they'd be halfway to their destination.

Lightning cracked outside. He thought he heard rain.

"Deal," he said.

August 10, 01:57

"How DID you get in?" Kate asked half an hour later—they'd searched the basement inch by inch to make sure there really wasn't another exit—pretty happy about getting her way. It wasn't every day that Parker McCall yielded to someone.

"Through the roof." He stood at the top of the staircase, pulled out his cell phone, opened it, then swore briefly. "Doesn't work down here."

He looked a lot cleaner than ten minutes ago. They had spent some time brushing soot off their clothes, off each other. That had been a picnic and a half. She'd just about jumped out of her skin when he touched her. It had taken everything she had not to let him see that he could still affect her with as little as a brush of his knuckles.

"Through the roof how?"

"From the next building. The rebels heavily secured the main entrances. Can't get in or out through there without a major fight. They were focused on that when I got here, hadn't gotten to securing the roof yet. I'm sure that has been done by now, but we'll fight our way out if we have to."

Fight. Oh God. She was scared stiff. Although if anyone could get her out of here, it was Parker. Especially this new, military version.

"How many are there?"

"Two dozen, tops. They're spread out over the four floors. Have to keep the whole building secured. They can't spare more than a handful for the roof. And up there, it's pitch-dark—a definite advantage."

For Parker. She, on the other hand, was afraid of the dark, especially when it hid murderous rebels. Parker looked…almost excited, as if this was nothing but a game.

"Are you going to tell me who you really are?" she asked.

He was Parker, but not *her* Parker. Not the man she had fallen in love with. This Parker was a lot darker and infinitely more dangerous. He moved with feline grace and constant preparedness. He had shot people without blinking an eye. She still couldn't process that.

He shrugged.

He'd always been darkly mysterious in a brooding-but-gorgeous kind of way, but now… "You—"

He had his hand over her mouth the next second, his hard body pushing her against the wall, into the shadows as he towered over her. But she didn't feel threatened, not for a second, never with Parker. She felt protected, but she wouldn't admit to herself just how much she had missed that. Voices filtered down from above.

They stood motionless, although since the stairs were made of stone, they didn't have to worry about creaking wood giving them away. But she barely dared to breathe, feeling paralyzed all of a sudden, and unsure if it came from the proximity of danger or the proximity of the man who had the power to liquefy her knees.

Parker ran a calming hand down her arm, which she didn't find calming in the least.

His skin still smelled the same—well, almost, plus hundred-year-old coal dust. On him, it smelled sexy. His body was still incredible, his lips still just as sensuous. He could still arouse her with a touch. The full-frontal contact was wreaking havoc with her senses.

And she panicked, because in her perfect little world, she had managed to convince herself that she was over him, that if they ever met again, she could walk by him without batting an eye. And here she was, assailed by such a sharp sense of longing it stole her breath away. It took all her willpower not to bury her face into the base of his throat and lap at the warm, smooth skin she knew she would find there.

The voices faded.

He didn't move.

And she didn't want him to.

No. Not again. She couldn't fall for him again. He had never truly loved her. He couldn't have. He had left her every chance he'd had. He had lied to her about things. She was pretty sure about that. She didn't want to think how many nights she'd lain awake wondering about where he was.

The two of them together spelled disaster, she reminded herself and pushed him away. Maybe with a little more force than was strictly necessary.

"Easy," he said, watching her with his usual unsettling intensity, as if trying to puzzle out her thoughts.

Not if she could help it. She stepped away from the wall. "Let's go."

He moved away from her with some reluctance. "I'll pick the lock, you see what else you can find here that we could use."

She moved around him and set to the task. The opposite wall of the staircase was lined with metal shelves. He already had a length of inch-wide nylon rope twisted around his waist that he had found, and a small screwdriver in his hand that he had gotten from the giant four-feet-by-four-feet toolbox near the bottom of the stairs.

The basement was used by the Russians as a storage facility. It held everything from broken office furniture to security supplies and crowd-control posts, even a crate of sea salt in one-kilo bags.

She opened an oil-stained box and rummaged through it. "What are we looking for exactly?"

"You'll know it when you see it," he said. "Grab anything you think we can use."

A lot of help he was.

But he was right. When she spotted the flashlight hanging from a peg behind the box, she took it. She was pleased to notice its metal case was heavy enough to be used as a weapon in a pinch. She flicked it on and grinned at the circle of light that appeared on the wall. "Even the battery works. Doesn't get better than that."

"Here we go." He straightened.

The door stood slightly ajar. He had obviously worked some magic on the lock.

"I don't even want to know where you learned that."

"Of course you do." He flashed a flat grin. "You want to know everything."

"Fine, I do. But I'm not asking. You wouldn't tell me, anyway."

His mouth twitched. "Wish we had time to look around some more, but we should probably head out." He bent his sinuous body into some SWAT-team pose.

Where had he learned that? Of course, she wasn't about to ask that, either. Trying to pin Parker down was futile. She ought to know.

He pulled the door a little wider, peeked out then closed it again, pulling his gun up and ready to shoot.

She could hear footsteps come their way then fade into the distance.

"Is your name Parker?" she whispered, unable to take her eyes off the weapon.

He tossed her a don't-be-stupid look that got her dander up, but then he nodded.

"You never were a foreign correspondent, were you?" Bits and pieces fell into place; a lot of things that had bewildered her in the past were making terrifying sense now.

He held her gaze. "No."

Oh God. "I've been so stupid, haven't I?" She looked away, embarrassed that she had never figured it out. He must have thought her incredibly gullible. She'd been blinded by love and lust. She would have believed anything of him. Not until the very end had she begun to see the chinks in his armor.

"You're one of the smartest women I know. One of the reasons why I fell in love with you."

Her heart, her stupid, gullible heart, turned over at his words. But had he really? Had he fallen in love with her, or had he been using her as some kind of a cover? He was a spy or a secret agent or something. He would probably say anything to have her cooperation so he could carry out his current mission successfully. She'd do well to remember that.

But it was difficult to remember anything when he put a hand on her shoulder. She shrugged it off. She didn't need to be further confused by the way his touch had made her feel. She hadn't been able to forget that, or anything else about him. Not for a single day, not even when she had dated other men.

"We'd better get going," she said, trying

hard to shake off the sharp sense of unreasonable longing that hit her out of the blue.

She needed to think about the hostages instead of Parker. They had to get to the gym before some rebels decided to check on their buddies stuck watching over the embassy staff. Every minute counted. Every minute could save a life.

He nodded slowly before he took his eyes off her and pushed the door open again. This time, the hallway must have been clear, because he stepped outside.

She followed. She had been a guest at the Russian embassy a half dozen times, but had never been in this part, wasn't sure of the way.

After a moment, Parker glanced back at her and parted his lips as if to say something, but was prevented by the sound of gunfire coming from somewhere above.

Above and to the left. They were just coming to a T in the hallway. There had to be a way to get up there. Kate turned left and took off running.

More gunfire. It lasted longer this time. Long enough to have killed every man and woman in the gym.

"Oh, God, no." She held the flashlight as tightly as she could, the only weapon she had, and ran faster, her heart beating its way out of her chest.

They had spent too much time arguing over what they should do. And now it was too late.

Chapter Three

August 10, 02:38

Kate resisted as Parker caught up with her and pulled her in the opposite direction.

"You promised to help." She tried to tug her wrist from him in vain.

"This way." He dragged her farther in the wrong direction, away from the sound of gunfire.

So he wasn't going to help the others. He had lied. The thought hurt, but she shook off the pain. She didn't have time for it. Of course he had lied. Just as he had lied to her about everything else. The only surprise was that she was still stupid enough to believe him. She would have thought she had grown wiser than that. Apparently not.

She had no idea who he was anymore, what he was capable of. Yes, he had promised to help, but he had promised other things before.

She dug her heels in, aware that if he decided not to listen to her, there was nothing she could do. He could and would take her out against her will. He'd always had a powerful physique and was in the same top shape now as he'd been two years ago, if not better.

In great shape, but in a terrible mood, not at all amused that she would stand up to him. Tough. He'd better get used to it in a hurry, because she wasn't the same woman he remembered. "We can't leave them to their fate."

He looked at her hard, harder than he'd ever looked at her before—scary hard. She couldn't breathe.

"I said we wouldn't. I don't go back on my word." He was practically growling.

But she obviously wasn't as smart as she had always thought herself to be, certainly not smart enough to take heed.

"Since when?" The question slipped out before she could have stopped it. He'd sure gone back on all his promises of love in a hurry.

And how embarrassing that after two years, she still wasn't over him, was still hung up on the past. Better make sure he didn't figure that out. "Sorry, this isn't about us." She tried to dance away from the subject.

He watched her with those laser-sharp, gunmetal-gray eyes of his for a moment. "Some of it *is* about us. But we'll have to get to that later. And we will."

His words sounded more like a threat than a promise.

"I'm sorry, Kate," he said then, and his face softened marginally before he looked away from her.

And damn him, her heart softened, too, which was the last thing she needed. She had to keep her wits about her.

"Why are we going in the opposite direction?" She was still suspicious.

He dragged her on. "We can't start an open battle where we're outnumbered twenty to one. If we do anything, it has to be guerilla warfare. Once again, here is what we are doing. I'm taking you out. Through the roof, if possible. We are going up. The hostages are on our way. I'll get them free of their guards and help them to the basement, where they have a chance to hide out until this is over. Even if they're found by the rebels again, they'll have a well-defendable position and I'll make sure they have some guns. That's the best we can do. The two of us sneaking out of here is going to be difficult as hell. Twenty people sneaking out is impossible. If we try, everybody dies. Do you understand?"

That made sense. She gave up resisting. He looked as though he knew what he was talking about, not that she was over the shock of his commando persona yet.

"I would appreciate if you didn't question every move I make," he bit out as they stole along the corridor in a hurry. "Our lives could depend on split-second decisions and your split-second responses."

"You think I'm putting us in danger by not following you blindly like some robot? Like you've given me reason to trust you and your almighty judgment in the past? Hardly."

His eyes flashed thunder. "Do you really want to get into all this right now?"

Okay. No, not really. She bit her tongue. Not at all. She would just as soon see their past buried if not forgotten. "What do the rebels want, anyway?"

"Probably troop withdrawal from their republic. They've been fighting for autonomy for the last seven years." He seemed to calm a little. "The violence slowed lately, since their leaders were captured, but apparently someone else has taken the helm." He thought for a second. "Strange, really, when you think about it. Their ethnic leaders are pretty divided. Some are turning into outright warlords. Mashev and his bunch." He shook his head.

"How on earth do you know all this?" She worked for the State Department and the Tarkmez struggle was barely a blip on her radar screen.

"CNN," he said, bland-faced.

"Yeah, right."

The corner of his mouth turned up in a grin.

"Not funny," she said, breathing a little hard since they were moving at a fair speed; it had nothing to do with his smile. Nothing whatsoever. "You have no idea how much I hate it when you lie to me."

His grin melted away, his face growing somber. "You have no idea how much I hate having to lie to you. Do us both a favor and don't ask me any more personal questions, okay?"

He was asking a lot.

"Are they going to get it?" She asked

something he wouldn't consider personal. "Their independence?"

"Not anytime soon," he said.

She didn't like the sound of that. It didn't bode well for the hostages. "How desperate are they?"

"Over a hundred thousand have been killed so far in the sporadic fighting. Women and children included." His gaze hardened. "Carpet-bombing is not an exact science."

God. She'd nearly lost it at the sight of Jeff going down, and the two dead rebels back there in the gym. She couldn't picture a hundred thousand dead. She blinked hard.

"They have nothing to lose," he added.

"I get it." When it came to fighting, which would probably come soon enough—either the French or the Russian government would try to get the hostages out—the battle would be savage. "Why isn't help here yet? Didn't anyone hear the gunshots? Didn't anyone call the police?"

"It's not a residential district," he said. "Nobody is here at night. And even if they were, the weather is drowning out most of the noise."

They turned down a hallway and rushed to the end, flattened themselves against the wall as Parker checked around the corner to make sure they wouldn't run into anyone that way. Then they were off again.

"Where is the rest of the embassy staff? The security?" he asked.

"Some of them were killed when the building was taken. I don't know about the rest. You think they were murdered, too?" She didn't even want to think about that.

"Probably. The rebels wouldn't want to leave anyone alive who might prove to be a danger later. They have the office and kitchen staff for bargaining. They would want to neutralize anyone trained to fight." He paused for a moment. "But if we knew for sure that some of the security staff are still alive, it would be worth spending time on finding them. We could use help with the hostages."

"If some of the security was still alive, where would they be?"

"Anywhere," he said after some thought, never slowing down. "There could be a man or two who had avoided capture, hiding out. Or there could be a few of them in the custody of the rebels, held in a different location from the rest of the hostages. Or they all could be dead," he added on a somber tone.

And since they were talking about missing

people, another thought popped into her head, and she couldn't believe that she had let it slip her mind earlier. "Where are the children and Tanya?"

He looked at her as if she'd gone off her rocker. "What children?"

"The ambassador and his wife have two girls. One's five, the other's seven. They were at the dinner. Wasn't that in your briefing?"

He swore under his breath. "My briefing was rushed. It focused on you and on the weak points of the building. When did you see the kids last?"

"At dessert. Then Tanya took them to some rec room to play. The nanny was supposed to watch them. The whole family was supposed to go home together later," she said miserably. But her mind was finally settling down enough to take stock of the situation. "I'm going to need a weapon." She eyed the rifle that hung from his shoulder and the handgun tucked into his belt.

"You have the flashlight," he said without looking back. "So there's a nanny, too? That's at least four civilians missing."

"I can shoot."

That gave him enough pause to slow and

stare at her, his dark eyebrows sliding up his forehead. "Since when?"

"Since I decided to take the consul position. U.S. embassies have been known for being attacked in the past. I've taken some firearm courses and a few months' worth of self-defense lessons."

Mostly she'd done it to set her mother's mind at ease. The consulate was in Paris, France, not in some third-world country. The worst crisis she had expected was an over-drawn credit card from too much uninhibited shopping.

For the first time, she was actually glad that she had a mother who saw doom lurking everywhere, and who had forced her to take extraordinary precautions. The only time, ever, when her mother's paranoia had failed was with Parker. She loved the man to death. Not a word of warning there, just when Kate would have needed it most.

They came to a row of doors and he tried the first. Locked. Tried the next one and the next one, too, before he found one that was open. He moved in low, the handgun held out in front of him.

"All clear."

She went in behind him and closed the

door. They were in a large storage room with nothing but boxes and boxes of what looked like reports and printouts.

"What are we looking for?" she asked when he began stacking some boxes by the wall.

"That." He nodded upward. "If we stay out in the open, sooner or later we're going to get caught."

She followed his gaze to the vent opening high up on the wall and swallowed. Another tight, dark place. She tried not to think of her great-grandmother's tiger-maple hope chest her cousins had locked her in for two terror-stricken hours on a hot summer afternoon when she'd been six.

"You'll be fine," he said.

Did he remember her telling him that story? That came as a surprise. He hadn't spent enough time at home during their year-long engagement to notice much about her. He certainly hadn't noticed that the relation-ship was falling apart. But, apparently, here and there on the odd occasion, he had actually paid attention.

"I'll be fine," she agreed, because she had no other choice. Whatever happened, she wasn't going to freak out, mess things up and jeopardize the lives of others.

Parker climbed his stack and had the cover off in seconds. He pulled himself up, half disappeared inside, then slid back out and dropped to the top of the boxes again. "Come on." He extended an arm to her.

She took it and ignored his hands moving lower on her body as he helped her to inch higher and squeeze in. The space seemed insanely small and devoid of air. She closed her eyes for a moment to calm herself. Parker's shoulders were much wider than hers. If he fitted, she had no reason to fear that she would be stuck. And there was air, there really was, she just couldn't draw it as long as fear constricted her lungs. All would be well as soon as she relaxed.

She inched forward, fighting the instinct to back out. And a few moments later Parker came up behind her. A barely audible rattle told her that he had put the vent cover back in place.

She swallowed, sweat beading on her forehead. *We aren't really locked in. We aren't locked in.* There had to be a hundred vent openings all over the building. A good kick and they could come out anywhere. She fought her panic with cold logic and won after a few seconds, then moved on, appreciating the fact that Parker hadn't said a word, hadn't rushed her.

"I'm going to be fine," she said again.

"I know." His hand came up from behind, pushing something her way. "Here, you take this."

The handgun.

She made sure the safety was on then slid it into her waistband. So he was going to treat her like a partner. That was certainly new. Maybe he had changed since they had parted ways. Yeah, and maybe pigs flied. In formation. At the Millville Wheels & Airshow he was so fond of.

She flicked on her flashlight, illuminating the dark passage ahead, not wanting to contemplate a new and possibly improved Parker. The old Parker had been enough to make her fall head over heels in love, had been enough to break her heart. She didn't want to think what damage he could do the second time around.

They hadn't crawled a full minute before Parker said, "Incoming call," behind her.

She stopped.

"Sir, we heard some shots from the north end of the building about five minutes ago. I also have information that the ambassador's children are in the building. Can you give us a location for the rec room?" he asked the caller. Then he listened before he swore under his breath. "The Colonel would like to speak to you," he said at last and handed the phone to her.

"This is Kate Hamilton."

"Glad to hear that you're well, Ms. Hamilton," a deep voice said without identifying himself. "I have my best man in there. You just do what he says. He's going to get you out as fast as possible."

Parker was the best man on his team? Well, he always was good at whatever he did. Except for the whole commitment thing.

"He'll take care of you," the man on the other end of the line continued.

"What is your plan for the other hostages?"

"The other hostages are not our responsibility. We have to trust them to the Russian forces."

"Who might be too late?"

"Ms. Hamilton—"

She cut the man off, not liking the tone he was taking. He might have been some military expert, but he wasn't here, hadn't seen the faces of those hostages. "If I see people about to be killed and there's a chance I might be able to help them that makes them my responsibility."

"Ms. Hamilton—"

"I do appreciate your sending Parker, though. We'll be out as soon as we can." She closed the phone and handed it to Parker, who was grinning like a kid at the circus, his face partially illuminated by the flashlight.

He looked breathtakingly gorgeous when he smiled. Not that the new Parker smiled all that much. But his smiles and those eyes had a way of breaking down her defenses.

"I can't believe you hung up on the Colonel." His grin widened another full inch. "I'm sure he can't believe it, either."

"You barely have any battery power left. We can't waste that on pointless arguments. So what did this Colonel tell you?" Whoever he was, she wasn't impressed. What kind of cold-hearted person would leave a group of defenseless people to their fate? *Politics.* She pressed her lips together.

"The Russian rescue team is here."

Her heart sped at the news. "Is that what the gunfire was about?"

"Their Alpha troops are in the process of securing the building from the outside. They are already on the roof. We have to get out before they storm the place and we get caught in the cross fire. A few of their Vymple special forces are coming, too. They won't be far behind."

"Can't we just all go to the roof? Then they can save us all?"

"To reach the Alpha troops, we'd have to get through the rebels. I'm not taking anyone into the cross fire. The roof is out. We have to find another way to escape. Before the Russians turn up the heat and attack full force. I don't want them to shoot any innocent people by accident."

She was trying hard to maintain a positive attitude about this whole mess, but it was slipping away from her as she listened to Parker. Sneaking out of here was already an impossible mission. Trying to help the other hostages while doing it added another level of difficulty. They really didn't need a timeline. "How soon will they attack?"

"They'll try to negotiate first. That can go on for as long as a couple of days, or they could lose patience with it in a few hours. We need to operate expecting the latter."

The whole prepare-for-the-worst thing. Made sense. She nodded, recalling a number of Russian hostage crises that ended badly for the hostages. "They'll probably shoot at everything that moves."

"I'm afraid so," he said.

"Okay, so we can't go to the roof."

"We'll find another way out after we get the kids and the hostages to safety in the basement."

"But we get the kids first?"

"Yes. We are on the same floor. It shouldn't take long if they are still where we expect them to be."

He didn't say, *and nothing has happened to them,* and she didn't dare to think it. She focused on the next step instead. "And help the other hostages."

He gave a low growl. "Would you like to save the ice cream from the freezer, too, so it won't spoil in case the Russians cut the power?"

"What? There's ice cream? Head to the kitchen first," she said, because she desperately needed a moment of lightness in the taut atmosphere.

"Tell you what. I'll take you for ice cream when we get out."

She couldn't see him, but just *knew* he was rolling those gunmetal-gray eyes. She didn't dare linger on the thought that he meant to take her anywhere after this was over.

"The Colonel said the rec room is in the west corner of the building," he said.

"Which way?" Inside the vent ducts, she was completely turned around and disoriented. Directions like east or west were beyond her.

"Turn left up ahead."

Not the best of news, since the sound of a small explosion had just come from that direction.

August 10, 05:40

WHEN THEY were in sections that opened to the various offices, their progress was excruciatingly slow; they stole forward at the rate of an inch a minute, never knowing who might hear them. But now they were finally in a section that had no openings to the outside, and could go faster. Kate kept the flashlight on. He didn't mind, knew she was uneasy with tight spaces and outright scared of spiders. The light reflected back toward him, however, did outline her body as she crawled in front of him. He didn't even try not to admire her curvaceous bottom.

He couldn't help the flashbacks of that

round bottom straddling him, images of Kate naked above him, the way he felt as he pushed into her soft heat, rising up to bury his face between her generous breasts.

"Parker?"

The insistent whisper brought him back to the present, although he noticed ruefully that one part of his body still lingered in the past and was bound to make the crawling more difficult. His body's reaction to her was instant and powerful. It had always been like that with Kate. "What is it?"

"Can you hear them?" She turned off the flashlight, but they weren't left in complete darkness, as some light filtered in through a vent cover up ahead.

Despite their situation, she was cool and collected. Almost as cool as she'd been when she had walked away from him two years ago, telling him that she had gotten a chance for the consul post in Paris and she was going to take it. She hadn't felt that what they had was enough to keep her with him.

And now for the first time, he wondered if he shouldn't have done something to stop her. *Stupid idea.* She was too nice. He was too dark. His life was— She was better off without him. *Safer.* The only mistake he had made had been asking her to marry him in the first place. That had been irresponsible, given his position. And yet, he couldn't regret it.

He took a few slow, controlled breaths and focused on the task at hand.

Men were talking up ahead, but he couldn't make out what they were saying. "Move closer. Careful."

But getting closer proved to be difficult, as the duct narrowed ahead. The building was an old one. Whoever had put in the system had had to adjust to some restrictions, he supposed, going around existing beams and structural elements.

Kate was nearly at the vent opening when she stopped. She looked back at him without saying a word. He could clearly hear the men below now, which meant they would hear Kate if she spoke. The best they could do was to communicate with hand signals. He did that, motioning forward.

Kate shook her head.

Okay, so she was stuck. Damn. They had to crawl back and look for another way. But first he wanted to take a look at the men below, see how many there were, how well they were armed. He listened. They were talking about Russian politics, not terribly useful to him at the moment.

He signaled to Kate to press herself to the side then moved up, parallel to her body. His face was in line with her ankles, then with her knees, her thighs. *Her hips,* heaven help him. He couldn't get as far as she had, his shoulders being wider. He got stuck with his nose about buried in her chest.

Her scent, her being, her energy surrounded him and filled him with a sharp longing that stole his breath.

She stayed absolutely still. Frozen. The men chatted on below.

He filled his lungs slowly and reached for his cell phone, set the camera on Record and handed it to her, pointing toward the vent cover. She only hesitated a moment before holding it up to a slot. Her breasts lifted as she stretched her arms.

He felt sweat bead on his brow. *Don't think about it.* He motioned to Kate to move the camera around a little. She did so, then when he signaled a minute later, she passed the phone back to him so he could view the file she'd just recorded.

He selected Play, then Mute.

Six men, their rifles propped against the

wall, hand grenades and handguns clipped to their belts next to their gas masks. One of them left, then came back in a few seconds. End of recording. Parker turned off the video as talk in the room switched to the expected harvest at the men's village. They cursed the Russian tanks that had destroyed half their fields.

He doubted he was going to find out anything important here in the near future, and they didn't have time to wait around and hope that the men decided to chat about more important things, such as where the rest of the rebels were and what their plans were for the siege.

He pocketed the phone and moved back a little, but she did, too, at the same time. And she had moved faster, bringing them face-to-face. The duct gave a low popping sound as both of their weights centered on the same spot.

The conversation stopped below.

He could see the sudden fear and questions in Kate's eyes. He put a hand on her arm. They just had to stay still for a while.

Touching her was a mistake.

The heat of her body seeped into his skin. He could smell her skin, her body lotion, which she had changed since they'd lived together, her shampoo, which was the same.

The men in the room resumed talking. He wasn't listening.

He could remember, as if it were yesterday, massaging that shampoo into her hair—she had worn it long back then. The two of them in the shower. Water sluicing over her curves, followed by his hands as they slicked over her soft skin, his mouth on hers, then on her neck, then everywhere.

"You're a maniac. We're going to break the stall." She had laughed, an indulgent look on her fine-featured, delicate face, water glistening on her long dark lashes.

"It'll be worth it." He'd reached under her buttocks and lifted her, pushed her against the tile wall then wrapped her legs around his waist.

She'd been ready, had always been ready for him, and he had pushed into her hot, tight, welcoming body, losing himself to the insanity of needing her more than the next breath he took.

Her low gasp brought him back to the present and he realized he had gripped her arm harder than he had meant to. Also, a part of his anatomy was pressed against her, making it pretty obvious what he'd been thinking about.

He was grateful that they couldn't talk so he couldn't be expected to explain. The pull of chemistry between them had always been unexplainable, anyway.

He couldn't see much in the dimly lit duct, but it sure looked as if her eyes were throwing sparks. Well, hell, as long as she was already mad at him…

He dipped his head forward and took her lips. She was soft and sweet, as mind-bending as he remembered. He had been craving this reunion from the day she had walked away. He liked to think that now and then she had thought of him, too.

So it came as a surprise when she put a hand to his chest and pushed, not even whispering, but breathing the words, "No. Parker, no," against his mouth.

And like the bastard he was, he kissed her anyway. Because he could.

And felt immensely gratified when in the next second she melted against him.

Chapter Four

She'd had this dream too many times, always woke with her body and soul full of aching and yearning. Except, this was no dream, as every cell of Kate's body attested. This was the real McCall.

Surprise had her resisting for an embarrassingly short moment, then pure gut reflex, body reaction, took over and all she could do was feel, all blood flow to her brain cut off. Minutes passed—not that she was aware of anything as mundane as the passage of time—before she could think again and pulled away. Breathing hard.

He came after her, but she turned her head—the small movement requiring an inordinate amount of effort—and those sensuous lips of his landed on her cheek. She became aware of his large hands that gripped her waist and had been inching upward. They stopped. Fell away.

I don't want this anymore, she wanted to tell him, but they couldn't talk, and even if they could, the words would have been a lie. She wanted him still. Her body throbbed with need from head to toe.

But her mind was emerging from its pleasure-induced stupor at last, and it reminded her that as spellbinding as the pleasure had always been with Parker, the pain of their breakup had been too devastating to bear.

She had given him her trust, her heart, her body and soul. She had believed with everything in her that he was *it,* the one for all time, the man to grow old with. Their breakup had caused her to lose not only her faith in him and marriage, but in herself, as well.

She bit her lip and squiggled down, anxious to separate their bodies. When her head was in line with the strong column of his throat, she tried not to think of how much she used to like to kiss that spot. Then came his wide chest and she blocked the memories of it rising above her, of how she would rest her head over it at other times and listen to that strong, steady heartbeat. The space was tight, but she managed to turn her head when she reached his flat stomach, hurried on as she moved lower, ignoring the all-too-obvious signs that he still wanted her.

Jason. She thought of one of the administrators at the embassy who had taken her out twice now to dinner. *Jason, Jason, Jason.* He was the same age as she, but with the heart of an old-fashioned gentleman. He was soft-spoken and into the arts. Had promised her tickets to Bizet's *Carmen,* the most popular French opera of all.

Jason left her pleasantly entertained and always looking forward to their next meeting. There was none of the mind-spinning heat that confused her and scared her so much with Parker, that had her acting out of character. Jason had not even asked for a goodnight kiss when he had escorted her home. And she found his patience and his European good manners admirable.

Focusing on him got her through crawling over Parker's body. For the most part. She drew her lungs full of air when there was finally a foot or so of distance between them.

She crawled in silence, up to the nearest intersection of ducts.

"Left," Parker murmured.

And she went that way, as fast and as

quietly as she could. Until she felt his hand on her ankle, his hot palm on her bare skin. Her pant legs had ridden up from crawling.

She couldn't deny the jolt. Did he— Then she heard footsteps from outside. She held her breath as men passed by them. When Parker removed his hand, a signal that she could move again, she resumed crawling until he told her to stop.

She reached a vent cover that looked out at a hallway and a door opposite. She crawled a few feet farther so he could look out, too. His bulk coming toward her in the narrow space should have made her feel more claustrophobic, but instead, she found his presence comforting.

"That's the rec room," he said.

She wasn't surprised that he'd been able to go right to it. He had a near-photographic memory. If someone had told him the building's layout, he would be able to navigate it as well as if he had a map in hand.

She drew a deep breath. The girls. *God, let them still be there and unharmed.* She pressed her lips together, forgetting everything else for a moment but the two sweet little girls with the big silk bows in their pigtails. "How do we get over there?"

But Parker was already laying down his rifle and reaching for the vent cover. He pushed it out, handed it to her. "I need the handgun."

He tucked the weapon into his belt, then squeezed through the hole, right arm first, then his head, then the left shoulder. She could barely hear the small thump when he dropped to the ground.

"Hold the cover back in place in case somebody walks by," he whispered when she stuck her head out to look after him.

She did that while watching him cross the hallway in two long strides and listen at the door. He had his gun in his right hand now, inching the door open with his left after a long second, keeping low to the ground. She wished she could point the rifle at the door and cover him if necessary, but since they were in a narrow section of the duct again, she couldn't turn the long weapon, couldn't aim it to where she should have.

Parker opened the door another inch. He could see in now, but she couldn't. She held her breath, desperately wanting to know what he'd found, but his body language gave away nothing. Then he turned a fraction and she could see the thunder on his face and the way his lips flattened into a grim line. Her heart stopped as he disappeared inside and closed the door behind him.

He wasn't going to say anything? He expected her just to sit there? She stared after him, stunned, and waited—not too patiently—a full minute. When she heard no sound of fighting, she eased the vent cover out of place and pulled it back in, slid it out of the way.

She considered the rifle for a second. She couldn't climb out with it; she needed both hands to manage that, and it was too big to stick into her belt. If she swung it over her shoulder, it would get caught and stuck in the small vent hole, and tossing it out ahead of her would have made too much noise. And she couldn't reach it after she slipped out. The vent holes were too high on the wall. Parker had to help her each time she had to get up there. She left it, knowing Parker wasn't going to be too happy that she'd abandoned one of their only two weapons.

She went out feet first, dangling from her fingertips soon and still a four-foot drop between her and the floor, thinking of her bad ankle, her most recent tennis injury. Putting out her ankle would be disastrous. She wasn't going to think about that. If she focused on something going wrong, for sure it would. She visualized landing with the grace of a ballerina then let go, tilting her weight so she would fall on her behind rather than on her knees if she toppled over.

She made more noise than had Parker, who was there the next second and dragged her into the room behind him, shutting the door quietly. A thunderstorm was brewing in his eyes.

"What do you think you are doing?" he asked through clenched teeth, the expression on his face making him seem a foot taller and much wider in the shoulders. He had looming down to a science.

Not that he could have scared her. Not Parker.

She was about to tell him to cut it out when her gaze caught on the body on the floor. "Oh my God." Her hands flew to her chest from where cold was spreading through her.

Tanya lay in a limp heap a few feet behind Parker, her throat cut, blood everywhere on the geometric-patterned carpet. Even in death, she had a determined look on her face.

Kate blinked as her stomach roiled, getting ready to reject the gourmet dinner she had eaten a few hours ago. Then Parker stepped in her view, blocking the gruesome sight, his hands coming up to her shoulders.

"Hey, take it easy." Concern replaced the earlier annoyance in his voice, the angry lines of his forehead smoothing out as he watched her. "You know her?"

She swallowed again. "She's the ambassador's wife. She was going to come back to dinner as soon as she handed off the kids to the nanny." Just a few short hours ago. Sure seemed as though a lifetime had passed since. "Where are the girls?"

She had hoped that they would find the children here with their mother and their nanny, had counted on it. Maybe under rebel guard, but here. It seemed a logical assumption since they hadn't been brought back to join the rest of the hostages at the gym. Every extra minute Parker and she spent wandering around the embassy, searching, decreased the chances of any of them making it out of here alive.

"Could have been taken someplace else. There are sixty-eight rooms and offices in the building, not counting storage closets," he said.

Her brain scrambled to come up with an idea as to where the girls might be, thinking of every area of the embassy that she had seen before. She tried not to think of how scared they probably felt, that there was a good chance that they had seen their mother killed. She absolutely refused to consider that the children themselves might not be alive.

The rebels wouldn't do that. They couldn't. These were innocent little girls, for heaven's sake. She wouldn't allow herself to remember the Russian school-hostage crises when hundreds of innocent children had died. She held Parker's gaze and believed with all her heart that he would find the children and save them. Because she had to.

She sank to her knees next to Tanya and raised a hand to the woman's face, gently closed her eyes. "You don't know how nice she was. She was so helpful with everything I asked. Just open and forthcoming and…" Her voice broke.

She reached for her top button, meaning to take her borrowed kitchen jacket off and cover the woman's face at least, but Parker put a hand on her shoulder.

"We can't. Have to leave everything the way we found it. If the rebels come back this way and figure out that there's someone loose in the embassy, they'll come looking for us."

Her hand fell away. "You think they have the girls?" she asked, but hoped with all her heart that the kids were hiding someplace with their nanny.

"They could still be here," he said, and squeezed her shoulders briefly before he let her go to look around again. He pointed at Tanya. "No defense wounds."

How could he tell with all that blood? She couldn't make herself look that closely. She shook her head as she got up, not understanding what he was getting at.

"Don't you think she would have defended the children? I would expect the body to be in the farthest corner, where she would have drawn back with them, shielding them behind her, fighting to the last drop of blood. But she was cut down right in front of the door, without defending herself."

"Almost as if she stood here, waiting for the rebels." She swallowed hard. "Trying to draw their attention to herself."

"Right." He was going for the armoire already and throwing open the doors. Not much there but video games, board games and books.

"But still, why wouldn't she at least go out fighting?"

He waited a beat before he answered. "She wanted to get it over with as quickly as possible. If she had the children hidden, she wouldn't want a prolonged fight. She wouldn't want to risk that the girls would cry out, or come out to help her. She wanted her attackers to spend the least amount of time in here."

His words painted a vivid picture she could only too easily imagine. She rushed to the built-in closet and found a hundred or so paperback novels in a messy jumble, her gaze returning over and over to Tanya. Where else could she have hidden two small kids? Her heart was pounding as she scanned the room, her gaze halting on the TV stand that had one of its doors slightly ajar. The piece of furniture was small and low to the ground, just large enough for a DVD collection.

The next second, she was crossing the room. She opened the door slowly and stared into a pair of round eyes that watched her, frozen with fear. The older girl. There was movement behind her.

Kate drew the first full breath of air since Parker had dragged her into the room.

"It's okay, Elena," she whispered as the

tension eased in her chest. They'd found them. The girls were here, unharmed. "Do you remember me? We had dinner together." According to their proud parents, the girls had an English nanny and a French babysitter who popped in when the nanny wasn't available. They spoke both languages, in addition to Russian, fluently.

Elena nodded slowly. Kate opened the other door and found the younger one, Katja, curled up asleep, her tear-streaked face squinched up as if she was anxious even in her dreams.

Then Elena looked behind Kate and screamed, waking the smaller girl, who started to cry immediately, repeating a single word, something that sounded like *matj,* which Kate thought meant *mother* in Russian.

"Shh." She reached forward to pull the girls out.

But Elena pulled back, holding back her little sister. "Mommy said we can't come out until she told us."

She couldn't force them, not even for their own good. They had to cooperate and do it quietly. "Your mom told me to come and get you if she got hurt."

Elena nodded. She understood that her mother was injured. "Did the bad people hurt her a lot?"

"Just a little," she said. "We have to go before they come back."

Elena eyed Parker.

"I'll move back," he said.

He had probably scared the girls; no wonder when they had witnessed a brutal attack by men in uniforms just like his.

"He is a friend." Kate wrapped her arms around the girls, who burrowed against her body, just about melting her heart.

Parker was talking in a calm, low voice a few steps away, in Russian. After a moment, that set the children somewhat at ease and the younger one peeked over Kate's shoulder at him.

"He's not going to hurt you. He is my friend. He is a very good man. He is going to take us from here so we'll be safe." She didn't let them go for a second, knowing that they needed the comfort of her touch.

Frankly, she needed theirs. She was a lot more freaked out than she let on.

But being responsible for someone else now gave her extra strength. Whatever came their way, she was going to tough it out for these girls. Strange how that worked. She wished she had the rifle Parker had left with her, and she knew that she would use it without hesitation when the time came. Nobody was going to hurt these kids while she was breathing.

"Do you know where your nanny is?" She tried to remember the name. "Have you seen Mrs. Baker?"

Elena shook her head. Katja was staring at Parker.

"She wasn't here when your mommy brought you up?"

The girl shook her head again.

"We have to go," Parker was saying.

And in a hurry, Kate thought. They couldn't be sure that nobody had heard Elena's scream.

"Let's go," she repeated to the girls, and stood, holding their hands, holding them close to her body.

"To daddy?" Katja asked, her incredible blue eyes still fringed with tears.

"Yes," she lied, her throat growing tight. They couldn't tell the girls the truth now. They needed them as calm as possible and moving fast. "We have to hurry so we can find him."

"What's wrong with mommy?"

Although Kate held the girls away from

the body on the floor, they must have seen it already from their hiding place.

"Did she die?" Elena asked.

And Katja's eyes were already filling up with tears all over again.

"She's just a little tired. We have to leave so that she can rest for a while," she lied again. They had to move in absolute silence. She had to make sure the children wouldn't cry and draw the rebels' attention. The girls would have to wait for the terrible truth until they were safely away from this place.

Elena was watching her doubtfully, but Katja nodded, and held her hand a little tighter.

The small gesture from the little girl who didn't know yet that she'd been orphaned and was all alone in the world again squeezed Kate's throat, sending moisture to her eyes. She glanced at Parker, caught a soft look on his face as he watched her. The same regret that clutched her chest swam in his eyes. He nodded as he went to the door and looked out. "Okay, hallway's clear."

Up until now, she had made sure that she'd been between them and the body on the floor, as had Parker. Now she turned them as they walked, talking about how quiet and fast they had to be to keep their attention on herself as they hurried out of the room.

Parker was standing below the vent cover. "You go back in. I'll take them to the basement."

The girls tightened their hold on her.

"I'll go with them. You can't just leave them alone while you come back up for the rest of the hostages."

"They've been alone for the past couple of hours. The basement is much safer than being up here. In another half an hour the rest of the embassy staff will be down there with them."

The girls pressed against her legs, one on each side.

He looked at them, and must have realized that he would need a crowbar to pry the kids away from her, because he shook his head, threw her a dirty look, then unfolded his fingers that had been waiting for her to step up to the vent hole, and jumped for it himself. He caught the edge on the first try, pulled out the rifle and then the vent cover and put it back into place.

"Are we going to stay out in the open now?" As much as she hated the ducts, she wasn't too crazy about the idea of wandering around in plain sight. "Where are we going?"

"Can't crawl in the walls with kids. They make one noise, it's game over."

And with a sinking heart, she knew he was right. "How far are we from the gym?"

"It's two corridors over and one floor up."

"We'll take the kids."

"They would have been safer sitting in the basement."

"Then I'll go and sit there with them."

"You are taking the shortest way out of here. I'm not letting you go in the opposite direction." And that was that, the look on his face said.

Fine. "Where is the staircase?" They'd taken so many turns in the ducts, she had no idea where they were anymore.

"That would be guarded by the rebels. And the elevators were taken out at the beginning, shut off along with the security system."

She tried to stay calm for the kids' sake. They were stuck out in the open, still with no clear plan on how to get out, two children in tow, no knowledge of where the main rebel force was hanging out and no way to get to the other hostages. Oh, yeah, and time was running out, too.

She didn't think things could get any worse.

But then a door opened, without any warning, not twenty feet down the hallway from them, and a scruffy rebel soldier stepped out.

SURPRISE FLASHED across the young man's face, but he was aiming his AK-47 already. Not fast enough. A barely audible pop, not louder than a person smacking his lips together, came from Parker's gun first. He loved the new silencer that the SDDU had been testing over the last couple of months.

One of the advantages of being a part of the Special Designation Defense Unit was that they got to try out all the latest gadgets first. He loved that part. And he loved knowing that he made a difference in his job. But he hated that a particularly gruesome mission in Southeast Asia had cost him Kate two years ago.

She gasped as the rebel soldier folded to the ground, but Parker was there already, catching the man's rifle before it could have crashed to the marble floor. Then he pushed through the door with his gun raised.

Nobody in there, he registered with relief.

He stepped back out, glancing at Kate, who had the kids behind her, protecting them with her body, blocking the sight of the fallen man. The girls were crying again, but at least quietly. She was talking to them in a soothing voice.

He grabbed the body by the boots and dragged it inside the room, scanned the place for all possible hiding spots and decided on a metal supply cabinet. He had to remove a shelf to get the guy in, but he managed, locked the door and pocketed the key. He didn't want the rebels to find the body and realize that there was someone inside the embassy who wasn't under their control. He didn't need them to organize a hunting posse. The man whose uniform he had taken earlier was safely stuffed into the vent duct near the gym.

Parker brought out the guy's gas mask and handed it to the older girl, hoping he could get his hands on another for the little one. Kate had worked her magic on them, it seemed, because they were no longer crying, just watching him with large blue eyes fringed with tear-soaked lashes.

They were cute and tough. Followed directions well. He supposed their life in a Russian orphanage hadn't been a bed of roses before their adoption.

"Everyone okay?" he whispered.

They were still too scared of him to talk to him. But Katja whispered something to Kate.

"She has to go to the bathroom," she said.

He tried to think when the last time was he'd seen one. Damn. Not anywhere nearby. He took in the kid's scrunched-up face. "Okay."

They found a bathroom without any problems. But then they spent an hour jammed into the same stall, balancing on top of each other as rebels came in and out. The girls kept as quiet as mice. He was simmering with impatience by the time they got out. Time, they'd only lost time, he reminded himself. They could have lost much more.

He moved ahead and glanced around the corner. All clear. He signaled them to follow. The elevator he'd been heading for stood a little over twenty feet away and was unguarded as he'd hoped. He'd figured nobody would care much about it since it was out of commission. Perfect for his purposes.

He walked up to the stainless-steel doors and pried them open with the knife he had gotten away from the first rebel he'd taken out. He pushed the panels aside enough for his head to fit in and looked around. The elevator car was stuck on the ground floor below them.

"Come on," he said as he stepped back and forced the door open another few inches, enough so he could fit in sideways. "We'll be going up through here."

Kate looked in and up at the metal ladder, holding the kids even closer. "Can they do this?"

He thought back to his own childhood. "Are you kidding? Kids climb like monkeys. Right?" He grinned at the girls and Katja smiled back shyly. She had a dusting of freckles across her nose and a very direct gaze that looked a lot like Kate's.

He lifted Elena first and placed her on the nearest rung of the ladder, wouldn't let go until she had a secure hold on the metal bar and started moving up. Kate went next so she could help the girl if needed. Then he helped Katja up and stepped in behind her, closed the elevator doors when they were all in, enclosing them in darkness. It lasted only a split second. Kate's flashlight came in handy.

He kept his attention on the three people in front of him as he climbed, careful not to rush them, although the pace was excruciatingly slow. But he didn't say anything, letting them pay attention to each handhold, each step. The drop to the top of the elevator was about twenty feet—probably not fatal, but enough to break a bone or two, injuries they could not afford. He watched them, all three, ready to catch whoever needed his help.

An old memory floated up from the dark recesses of his mind. His father teaching him how to climb a tree in the park. He couldn't have been more than four at the time. It'd been well after midnight. Then the picture switched to the last time he'd seen his father. He hadn't thought about his old man in a while, hadn't had that nightmare in a decade or more. He pushed those thoughts away.

When they reached the door that led to the second floor, he motioned for them to go a little higher until he was level with it. He pressed his ear against the metal panels. No sounds came from outside. He eased them open an inch, looked out, but couldn't see anyone. He opened the doors wider, stuck his head out first then his body. Luck was still with them. He helped the others out.

"Which way?" Kate asked once the doors were closed behind them.

The girls didn't look too shaken by the climb. They were more excited than anything else at this point, actually, and he was grateful for the short attention span of kids that age.

"We're going to sneak around a little," he told them.

"Like Super Spy Girls on the Cartoon Channel?" Elena's face was glowing.

He had no idea what she was talking about. "Exactly," he said.

He shut his eyes for a second and pictured the hallways they had taken on the floor below. Where did that put them in relation to the gym? "This way," he said and they followed without another word.

This hallway was not decorated with paintings and even the light fixtures were utilitarian, a stark contrast to the antique chandeliers of the main areas of the embassy. He glanced at the row of doors on each side. Maybe these were the back offices where visitors weren't allowed. He tried a door. Locked. Not that he wanted to go in there, but he wanted to make sure nobody would be coming out and getting behind him.

Then, at the next door, he heard a small noise and he froze with his hand on the doorknob. He motioned for Kate to stay back and stay down with the children. Since the embassy was furnished mostly with antiques and had kept the old style, he wished they had kept the antique hardware, too, with keyholes instead of security locks. That way he could have taken a look. Going into a situation he knew nothing about was dangerous, but he had no other choice. If there were rebels in there, he had to neutralize them.

Kate was holding the rifle in front of her. The girls were crouched behind her, peeking over the side, watching him, wide-eyed. He'd better not make a false move. Whatever waited for him behind the door he would deal with it. Whoever was in there and however many of them there were, he would not allow them to reach Kate and the kids.

He tried the knob silently and wasn't too surprised when it gave. He opened the door a millimeter. He was ready to shoot at anything that moved, but nothing did. A dozen bodies covered the floor. They weren't wearing the camouflage militia outfits of the rebels, but the official Russian dress uniforms. The embassy security force, all dead and piled on top of each.

He stepped in carefully but stuck a hand back out the door to signal to Kate to stay where she was with the girls. They didn't need to see this. He spotted a man in civilian dress, too, with a different style of military haircut and typical Midwest good looks, ruined only by the hole in his head. He figured him for Kate's bodyguard. The muscles tightened in his face. He stepped farther inside and grabbed as many guns and gas masks as he could for the hostages, then drew back in surprise when one of the men he touched groaned. Parker had his gun aimed at the guy's head the next second.

"Help," the man begged in Russian, his unfocused eyes fluttering open.

He had blood on his face, but Parker couldn't see an open wound. The guy had plenty of blood soaking his pant leg, too.

"Can you stand?" Parker asked and held his left hand out, keeping the gun handy in the right.

The man rubbed the back of his head. "Give me a second. I got knocked out." But he was scrambling to his feet anyway. He looked at the carnage around him, his eyes and the set of his mouth hardening.

"What happened?" Parker asked.

"I don't know. I was at the back gate. We got ambushed." Anger seethed in his words. "They must have thought I was dead and brought me here." He pressed a hand to his leg and limped over a body, stared at the carnage. "They killed everyone."

The man eyed Parker's uniform warily. "You're not one of them. Alpha troops?" he asked with suspicion. "Did they take the building back?" He seemed angry at the thought. Probably because he had missed the action. Protecting the embassy was his duty, and here he'd lain the whole time, out cold.

"I'm a friend of the ambassador. I was here for dinner. The Alpha troops are on the roof, negotiating."

The man looked him over, glancing at the rifles slung over his shoulders. "I'm Ivan. Let's do what we can from in here." He reached for a rifle.

Parker pretended that he didn't see the move as he kept surveying the room.

"Can't take offense, I suppose," Ivan said good-naturedly, seeming to marginally relax at last. "I don't trust you, either."

Parker kept an eye on the guy as he turned to leave, switching to English when they were out of the room. "I have the ambassador's children and their nanny."

The man took in Kate, hesitated for a moment. "She's not the English nanny."

A tension-filled moment passed.

"She's the new one," Parker said. "She came today to start training to replace the other one. She hadn't been introduced to the staff yet." He didn't trust the guy with Kate's true identity. He didn't trust anyone just now.

Ivan accepted his explanation with a nod. "Where are we going?"

"The other hostages are in the gym."

At least he hoped so. He had told them to stay put when he'd left them. The liberating forces were on their way to them. Even if the rebels came looking, the hostages could defend a barricaded room a lot easier than they could defend themselves if they were caught out in the open. And breaking out of the embassy wasn't a possibility for a large group like that, even with the guns they had. Too many rebels secured all the exits of the building.

The sound of gunfire came from the roof, a short burst, then silence. Both Ivan and Parker pulled back into a protective position around Kate and the children. A moment later, when nothing else happened, they both stepped away, ready to move on.

"How do you plan on liberating the hostages?" Ivan asked.

"I have a plan," he said simply.

"I can help."

Yes, he could. Parker watched the cautious expression in the man's eyes. It had been this guy's job to keep the embassy safe and he had failed. That had to burn him. He would probably do anything to redeem himself. And Parker had to trust him because he needed help, badly. He handed him one of the handguns.

"We are taking the hostages to the basement where we can barricade ourselves until the embassy is taken back." He felt no need to mention his other set of plans for Kate and himself. His orders were to get Kate out.

The man considered his words for a moment then nodded. "I'll go ahead and make sure the way is clear."

But Parker had another idea. He'd been uneasy about having the children around, taking them into a potentially explosive situation. There was a chance that the hostages had been recaptured in the short time he and Kate had been gone. There might be a fight waiting for them. Better to have the girls as far from that as possible.

"How are your arms?" he asked Ivan.

"Fine." The man pulled himself up straight, wanting to prove that he was capable, probably desperate to look strong enough for whatever Parker had in mind.

"Can you take the girls to the basement and barricade the door down there?"

The man only hesitated a moment before he nodded. "But if I barricade the door, how will the rest of the hostages get in?"

"Same way you will." They reached the coal-chute grid and Parker pulled it off then began to unravel the length of rope from around his waist.

Kate threw him a questioning look, but didn't argue with him for once. She knew as well as he did that the longer they had the kids out in the open, the more likely it was that they would run into some rebels who wouldn't care who got killed when they opened fire. He hated to let the girls go as much as Kate did, but it would have been insane to drag them along on this dangerous mission.

She bent to the children and began explaining to them what was going to happen and what they needed to do. They seemed okay with it. The sight of the security uniform seemed to have set them at ease with Ivan. They probably saw men in the same uniform every day and knew they were with someone who would protect them.

Kate hugged and kissed them both

before lifting Elena onto Ivan's back and Katja into his arms. "Hang on tight. Super Spy Girls, remember?" She gave them an encouraging smile.

They didn't exactly smile back, but at least they weren't crying. They went in, Ivan hanging on to the ledge while Parker screwed the grid back into place then tied the rope to it. Then Ivan could finally move over to the rope and begin his descent.

"They'll be fine, right?" Kate's emerald gaze searched Parker's for reassurance.

"The basement is the safest place for them right now. And they have an armed guard, a professional." That was as good as he could arrange under the circumstances. "I'll go keep watch. Let me know when he yanks on the rope." He strode to where the corridor turned, keeping lookout.

"Okay," Kate called in a whisper a few endless minutes later.

Parker glanced at his watch. Ivan had made good time. The embassy guards obviously kept in top shape. He walked back to Kate, untied the rope and looped it around his shoulder, then they headed toward the gym together. They were almost there when he heard footsteps from around the next bend.

Grateful that the girls had gone, he stopped and listened carefully. Only one man, he registered with relief. That was the good news. He glanced around the corner quickly. The bad news was that the guy was heading for the gym. But it wasn't the worst part by far. Parker swore under his breath. The man had a belt of explosives strapped around his midriff.

And if the rebels had *one* guy walking around as a human bomb, they probably had others.

Chapter Five

Kate held her breath, knowing there was someone in the corridor in front of them, knowing Parker was about to confront the man. They had managed to stay alive so far. She prayed that their luck held out.

Then she stared as Parker pulled his knife, but instead of lunging forward and around the corner, he cut a line across his left palm, pumped his fingers a couple of times to get the blood going. He lifted his right index finger over his lips to tell her to be quiet before he smeared blood on his face, covering his features almost completely, and staggered out into the open.

He moaned something in Russian or Tarkmezi—she couldn't tell the two languages apart—and an urgent response came. Then there was silence.

"All clear," Parker said next.

By the time she peeked out, he was wiping his bloody face on his sleeve. Then he cut off a strip from the dead man's shirt and bandaged his self-inflicted wound with speedy efficiency before she could even think about offering help. Frankly, at this point, she wouldn't have been surprised if he'd got out some commando first-aid kit and sewed himself up.

"Stay in cover," he mouthed as she caught up to him.

She didn't like the idea. She had a rifle and she knew how to shoot. She wanted to help, to even the odds a little. They were in front of the gym's door.

"What are we waiting for?" she whispered back.

He tapped his index finger to his ear.

She didn't hear anything. Then she got it, that was exactly what he was worried about. Everything was quiet inside. Either the hostages were dead, or under guard again and forbidden to speak as before, or they had heard the exchange of words outside and were preparing to shoot the living daylights out of the rebels they expected to enter any second.

"Vents?" She pointed down the hallway where there was a vent cover. They could climb up and take a look inside the room without its occupants noticing. She couldn't believe she was suggesting crawling back into the dark, tight place. But it seemed a better solution than to walk into a situation blindly.

Gunfire sounded from the roof again. Or maybe closer. Could be the Russians were inside already.

"No time," Parker told her, probably thinking the same, then called out something that she figured was the Russian version of, "Hold your fire."

He tried the doorknob. Locked. He shouted something else. A response came, then more conversation back and forth, followed by the sounds of something heavy being dragged away from the door. Then it opened, the barrel of an AK-47 poking out.

April 10, 10:15

"YES, COLONEL." Parker spoke into the phone.

He was back in the vent system with Kate again, having seen the hostages safely to the basement through the coal chute. With Ivan to organize them and the guns and gas masks he'd been able to give them, they should be able to defend themselves if everything didn't go according to plan.

He still had about ten percent battery power left in his cell, and he'd figured he'd better check in with the Colonel since the location of the hostages had changed. He wanted someone to be aware of that, in case the information could be passed along to the Russians.

"They should be as safe as possible. They are armed and hidden in a well-defendable position. They have a Russian security guard with them."

"You're sure about the explosives?"

"I can be sure only about the one I've got here." He carried the belt of TNT slung across his shoulder. "But my gut instinct says there's more."

"Get her out of there."

"Yes, sir." He sure was working on it.

"There's a press conference called for noon. I expect the Russians will come clean about the embassy crisis to us before that, then the CIA can offer help. Not that they'll take it, dammit."

The Colonel wasn't a swearing man, even frowned on the practice among those who reported to him. His frustration was a reminder of just how dire their situation really was.

"What's your next move?" he asked.

"I'm gonna try to get into the security office and bring the security system back online for a few minutes. If I could figure out what positions the rebels are holding, I could map a way out."

"I have a brand-new blueprint of the embassy in front of me that just came in. Where are you now?"

"Second floor, a hundred feet or so east of the gym, in a vent duct that's running parallel to a hallway to some inner courtyard."

"Okay," the Colonel said. "As soon as you can go down, do it. The security office is to the southeast of you, one floor down."

"Roger that," Parker said and signed off. He was coming to a passage where the duct narrowed again and he needed his hands stretched in front of him to wiggle through. He pushed his guns and the TNT belts in front of him.

"Can you make it?" Kate asked from behind him. They were once again in a section where there were no openings to the duct so they could talk a little more freely as long as they kept their voices down.

"Squeaking by."

Silence stretched between them as he got through the tough parts.

"This is what you've been doing all along, isn't it?" she said out of the blue as she eased her smaller body after him without any trouble.

He knew she wasn't talking about worming through ventilation systems. She was talking about his job. Hell of a time to bring up the issue.

He could have pretended that he didn't know what she meant, but he would only insult her intelligence and tick her off. Kate didn't take well to being patronized. "I can't discuss my job with anyone. Not even with my fiancée." He glanced at her.

"Ex-fiancée," she corrected tartly.

There was a hardness to her now that hadn't been there when he had met her, and he regretted that most likely he had brought about the change.

"I'm sorry," he said, and found that there was a long list of regrets behind that sentiment, a list he had no time to detail or even think about right now.

"No, fine. You're right. It doesn't matter. None of what happened matters, anyway."

She sounded tired and maybe a little defeated.

He wanted to protest that it did matter, hating the dejection in her voice even more than he hated the hardness of her words. And he couldn't even see her face because she was behind him. He couldn't grab hold of her shoulders and make her look at him, make her listen while he explained everything, because he could not give any explanations.

He had requested permission, back when he had first realized that he was falling in love with her. His request had been denied. Their life together had been based on lies. He had thought that the fact that their love was true would be enough, that it would cover everything. It hadn't.

He reached a three-way junction in the vent system with one branch going to the floor below them. "I'll slide down. Give me a minute before you come after me," he said. He wanted to make sure the route was passable before both of them got wedged in.

He'd had a friend when he'd been in the army who was into caving and had taken him and a few others spelunking. This place had reminded Parker of that, the tight spots and turns, the semidarkness, the seeming lack of air. Except that in the caves you could make all the noise you wanted without having to fear you'd be shot at.

He cleared the bend. "Okay," he whispered back to Kate.

They were coming into a stretch with a number of openings so they wouldn't be able to talk. He stole forward to the first, eager to be able to look out.

An empty office.

He moved on and tried the next. Damn. "Found the nanny," he whispered.

"Alive?"

He shook his head, looking at the stout Englishwoman sprawled on the floor. Looked as though she had put up quite a fight. The room's antique secretary desk had been reduced to kindling.

He moved up to the next room. Empty. Same with the next and the next. He was nearing the end of the duct and a sharp turn he wasn't sure he would be able to navigate by the time he finally found what he was looking for—the security office.

But of course, since everything that could go wrong on a mission usually did, this room wasn't empty. A rebel soldier sat in front of the rows of darkened monitors, snoozing.

Parker focused on the familiar-looking wide canvas belt around the guy's waist. Another human bomb. Just what they didn't need.

"Someone's in there," he breathed the words toward Kate, couldn't be sure if she heard him or even saw his lips move as she had the flashlight turned off.

He kept his attention glued to the room, couldn't see all of the space from his vantage point, couldn't see if there was anyone in there with the man, so he waited. No sounds of anyone moving around. Gunfire came again from somewhere far above. Didn't seem to be any closer than the short bursts they'd heard before.

Didn't look like the Alpha troops were making much progress. Or could be that they were engaging the rebels up there only as a distraction and were working their way in someplace else entirely. That was what Parker would have done. Machine-gun fire peppered the silence again. The man slumped in the chair didn't wake, didn't even stir.

Parker turned on his cell-phone camera and stuck it out through the vent cover's slots, tilted it down as best he could without risking dropping it, careful not to scrape against the vent cover and make noise. Then he pulled the cell back to look at what he got. Nothing. Perfect. Their man was alone, which he indicated to Kate by holding up his index finger in the spot where the light coming in from the vent hole made it visible.

He could barely see her silhouette in the darkness, but thought she nodded.

He pulled his handgun and slowly pushed the silencer through the slot, took careful aim. He couldn't give the man a chance to shout out. They had no way of knowing who might be nearby. So he aimed for the head, knowing it would make the hit messy, but unable to think of another solution that would take care of their problem as quickly and efficiently.

A small *pop* came first, then a louder thud, as the rebel hit the floor. Parker waited but there was no sound of any commotion from outside, no sign that anyone had heard. He pushed the vent cover out, held on to it so it wouldn't clang to the floor, and squeezed his shoulders through the opening, then helped Kate.

"Don't look," he said, too late.

Her face was already white, her eyes round with horror. Head shots were always messy and this was no exception.

"It had to be done. Him or us," he tried to explain, fearing that she was beginning to see him as some sort of a monster, unsettled by the thought that if she did, she might be right. If it had just been him, he would have killed the man without thought. Only because she was with him had he hesitated at all.

"I know." Kate reached a hand to his arm in a brief touch of reassurance.

What did she know? He looked at her and saw the understanding in her eyes, was humbled by it. Yeah, she knew.

And he found he breathed easier all of a sudden. "Why don't you check on the computers?" He pushed her toward the nearest desk gently, wanting to turn her from the gruesome sight and give her mind a chance to be busy with something else.

He checked a smaller door in the back. "There's a bathroom in here." He looked around to make sure it was safe and nearly got knocked over when Kate whizzed by him, then shut the door in his face.

He allowed a small smile before he walked back to the man and removed the TNT belt. When he was done with that, he tugged off the guy's camouflage jacket and covered his head with it. He didn't take the man's guns, only his ammunition. They might need serious firepower on the way out.

He used the bathroom after Kate was done and had returned to the computers. Then he came back out for the dead man, got him into the chair and wheeled him inside one of the stalls and closed the door. When he was done, he washed his hands and face, drank.

Most of the PCs and monitors had bullet holes in them. She was rebooting one of the unharmed computers by the time he came out. He watched as a gray screen came up. Password-protected, of course. He swore under his breath.

He wasn't bad at cracking security, but he wasn't a whiz, either—it wasn't his specialty—and he figured the security PCs at the Russian embassy had to have some pretty fancy systems. He had no time to waste by fooling around on a prayer of a chance. Instead, he dialed the Colonel.

"I'm going to need a computer expert on the line," he said. "Is Carly available?" Carly Tarasov was a new member of the SDDU team, the wife of one of Parker's old buddies, Nick, who'd met her on a mission and promptly recruited her. With good reason. She was a genius when it came to encryption codes.

"You got it. Give me a second to reach her. I take it you got in?"

"Yes, sir. Found more explosives, too."

Silence at the other end.

"One more thing, sir."

"Whatever you need."

"I need permission to disclose."

Longer silence this time.

"She has security clearance, sir," he reminded his superior officer.

"Not this high," he said. "Her boss's boss doesn't even know that the SDDU exists." The Secret Designation Defense Unit was normally used in clandestine missions that skirted Congressional approval, running operations where to take out a dangerous enemy, they often had to bend the rules of the game.

"With all due respect, sir, her boss's life is not on the line."

The Colonel grunted. Another moment of silence followed. "The most bare-bone basics only," he said finally. "Just what she's likely guessed on her own by now. Nothing but what she absolutely must know to cooperate and survive."

Parker's chest expanded, and his gaze

locked with Kate's. She was watching him and listening with interest. "Yes, sir. Thank you, sir," he said.

HE WAS finally going to tell her what was going on, was finally going to let her in. She didn't know whether to be relieved or scared. Scared that she would find out that she had made some bad decisions in the past and had judged him unfairly.

She spoke before he had the chance to. "You didn't just start this job, did you? This is what you did, even back when we were engaged and living together." Nobody got to be this good without years of experience.

She waited, afraid now that she'd spoken that he would dodge the question, as he had dodged her questions in the past.

But he nodded.

She drew a deep breath, her mind going a mile a minute. Here it was, the truth coming out, finally. She owed him her own part.

"You know those times when you were gone and I couldn't reach you? Sometimes I thought that you had somebody else."

Thunder came into his eyes. "You thought I was cheating on you?" His voice was dangerously low.

She nodded tentatively, licking her lips in a nervous gesture.

His eyes flashed. "You said you loved me. How could you not trust me at all?"

Was that hurt in his voice?

"You said you loved me. How could you lie to me the entire time?"

That gave him something to think about. He held her gaze, a storm of emotions simmering under the surface.

"What was I supposed to think? You were moody a lot, you know, when you came back from assignment." Her voice choked. "And your shirt smelled like perfume sometimes."

"I work undercover. Sometimes I work with others. There are a few women on my team." His voice was husky, toe-curlingly sexy.

She wrapped her arms around herself. "Why not tell me at least that? That you worked some law-enforcement job you couldn't tell me more about. I could have accepted it." At least, she thought she could have.

"I had no authorization. When we met, I was investigating an information leak that had some clues pointing to the State Department—where you worked and still work," he emphasized.

That gave her pause and brought up more questions than answers. "Did you ask me out to get information from me? Was I your cover or something?"

He stepped closer, his eyes holding her in such a stark bind that the room around them seemed to disappear. She couldn't look away.

"When you backed into my car—" He paused and her heart sank.

She remembered the accident clearly. She'd been distracted, leaving the parking lot of the Harry S. Truman building, that is, the headquarters of the U.S. Department of State. A few blocks from the White House in Washington, D.C., it was in a neighborhood called—no joke—Foggy Bottom.

"I was there watching someone. I couldn't be sure that you didn't make me miss my man on purpose," he said.

She felt cold. He had only asked her out that night to investigate her. And she had been completely taken in by him. The attraction, on her part, had been instant. There he was pretending and, oh God—she had *slept* with him. Anger and embarrassment swept over her.

"I'd run a background check on you by the time we met for dinner. I knew you were clean. I could have skipped," he was saying. "I went— And you were—" He shook his head. "I didn't see *that* coming."

She was still angry, but she wanted to hear him out. She wanted to be fair. It seemed she might have made some rash judgments in the past. They had cost her. She didn't want to make the same mistake now—didn't want to be ruled by her rush of emotions.

"I wanted you from the first second I saw you," he said, carefully enunciating each word. "When I found out where you worked, I told myself I had to walk away from you. But I couldn't."

Judging by the harsh intensity on his face, she didn't think he was lying. Some of the tension inside her chest eased.

"But don't you think you should have told me at least some of the truth after the engagement?" She wasn't ready to give in yet to the dizzying pull that drew her to him, had always drawn her to him.

"I wanted to. I didn't get the authorization. I wanted to put off asking you to marry me until I could come clean. It just— Things got away from me."

Yes, she remembered. Things had gotten

away from both of them. They had been explosive together from day one. Dynamite. They couldn't get enough of each other's company, bodies. From their first date, she could think of no other man.

"You let me go without a word." That had hurt. Even at that point, she had still hoped that something could be worked out if they both wanted it enough. She had expected him to try to keep her, had hoped he would heed the wake-up call. Instead, he had let her go without a fight. Which she took as a sign that he hadn't really loved her at all.

"What did you expect from me?" he asked, tight-lipped, going very quiet.

Parker in quiet mode wasn't a good thing.

"I expected you to give me a reason to stay."

He turned away before she could have caught the expression on his face, walked to the blank computer screen and stared at it.

"Remember Jake Kipper? He stopped by one night with some car parts for me."

She did. "Yes." There hadn't been too many people in Parker's life it seemed. His parents were gone and he had no brothers or sisters. Only a handful of friends stopped by now and then, and out of those, she had only met Jake that one time. He had an infectious grin and had brought his wife along, a woman who clearly adored him.

She'd been insanely young—too young to be married, early twenties at the most—beautiful and happy. The same happy Kate had hoped to be in her own marriage with Parker. Well, *that* didn't happen.

And Jake and Elaine had died in a car accident a few months after that, the news sending Parker into one of his dark moods for weeks.

"The group I work for—" Parker drummed his fingers on the desk, his muscles tight, his face hard. "Nobody's cover had been broken before. Jake was the first and so far the last."

Her breath caught. "Are you saying—"

"It was a car bomb, Kate, not an accident." Pain and regret swam in his gaze. "Elaine was pregnant."

Her hand flew over her mouth. "You didn't tell me."

"It was still early. I don't think they'd told anyone yet. It came out in the autopsy."

Other things clicked into place. How Parker had said it was too early for a baby when she'd told him she'd like to start trying as soon as they were married. She had taken that as yet another rejection.

For the first time, she had to consider that maybe he'd just been scared. Hard to think of Parker like that. He was never scared of anything.

She shifted toward him. He waited, not moving a muscle, so still she thought he might be holding his breath. She stepped close, then closer, putting her arms around his torso and burying her face at last into the crook of his neck, inhaling his scent, the warmth of his body. And then his strong arms wrapped around her and held her tightly.

Moisture gathered in her eyes. God, she had missed this. Missed him.

"I was scared to death that I couldn't keep you safe." His voice sounded scratchy.

"Looks like I found plenty of trouble without you," she said ruefully.

"I'm here now." He lifted a hand to tuck her hair behind her ear, put a finger under her chin to tilt her face to him. "I'm not going to let anything happen to you, Kate."

She knew. And her heart leaped against her rib cage because she also knew that he was going to kiss her. His gaze was dropping to her lips already.

"Parker, we…" she started to say, but then changed her mind and rose to meet him halfway.

He kissed her so sweetly, so tenderly, as if he had put all the longing of their separation into that one kiss. Her body responded on autopilot. Nobody had ever gotten to her the way Parker did without half trying. He was the only person that she had ever slept with on a first date.

Her hands crept under his shirt. She needed to touch his skin, needed to feel the familiar landscape of his abdomen and his chest, needed to feel that he was still the same. Her Parker.

The thought pulled her back from the haze of pleasure and she untangled herself from him shakily, finding the strength somewhere to step away.

He wasn't her Parker. He was no longer her fiancé. And if things were the same, they wouldn't work, anyway. They hadn't worked in the first place. Truth was, beyond the physical, they had failed to make their relationship a viable union.

Now she knew what he did for a living. But she didn't know yet how she felt about that. She wouldn't be any happier with him being gone half the time now than she had been before. And he could never tell her everything. There would always be secrets between them. That wasn't her idea of marriage.

"Kate." He reached for her.

She drew back. "I'm sorry."

He gave her a rueful smile. "Let's call a moratorium on apologizing to each other, okay?"

She nodded.

"Do you have any more questions about me? There are at least a few things now that I could tell you."

But she shook her head. She knew enough. And what she really wanted to know, anyway, was whether he still loved her.

Did she still love him? Hard to say when the need for his touch still hummed through her body. For the moment, the physical pull still obscured the emotional side of things.

She didn't want to love him. She knew that without a doubt. She didn't want to open herself up to a world of hurt again. She had found out enough about him now to give more meaning to the events of their past, lay it to rest somehow and hope she could finally bury her regrets along with it.

"I think—" She didn't get to finish what

she was saying. They were interrupted by his cell phone.

"Okay, go ahead." Parker put the phone on speaker then laid it next to the keyboard as he dropped into a chair.

"Hang on for a second." It was the Colonel. "Before I hand you over, you should probably know that the rebels have made another demand. In addition to troop withdrawal, they also want some Tarkmez war leaders released. There's a trial coming up soon at the international court at The Hague. All right, here's Carly."

"Hey, beautiful," Parker said with a half smile and Kate's stomach clenched.

"Sucking up right off the bat, huh? Must be in a lot of trouble, McCall."

"Nah. Just wanted to hear your sweet voice. How's the baby?"

"Intent on kicking his way out. As stubborn as Nick. You know what I'm talking about?"

"Hear you about that," he said, then briefly ran through his problem. "You think you can help me?"

"I have to, don't I, if I want a godfather for this kid," she groused good-naturedly.

And Kate relaxed.

She was beginning to suspect that Parker had a slew of friends she hadn't been allowed to meet because they worked for the same group or organization or commando patrol or whatever it was he belonged to.

"I'll stand guard by the door," she whispered, not wanting to interrupt.

Parker nodded. They set up a voice connector on the computer to save his cell-phone battery as much as possible, then started the work with Carly, and between the two of them, a grainy image flickered onto the screen after a couple of hours. Kate had spent that time listening at the door, peeling her ears for any noise that might indicate that rebels were coming their way.

"How about the rest? I can only see with one security camera," he said toward the phone.

"We have to reroute the feed from the others to the one working monitor you have. Then you should be able to scroll through the images," Carly told him, and they got working on that right away.

Three more nerve-wracking hours passed before they got anywhere. Some of that time Kate spent by taking a sponge bath in the bathroom sink, with the dead body locked in the stall behind her. She tried not to look at the feet in the mirror.

But finally they did have the pictures, one hallway after another, the front entrance, the back, Parker flicking through them one by one.

"Thanks. Does Nick ever tell you that you are as brilliant as you are beautiful?"

"Not enough. He's barely home," she said then went on with some admonitions about Parker proceeding very carefully.

So she was very pregnant, close to birth from what she'd said, and her husband, who seemed to be on the same team with Parker, was obviously off on some mission. Yet it didn't seem to bother her. There had been humor in her voice when she'd brought it up and an enviable amount of love.

And Kate wondered if she could ever be like that, if what Carly had would ever be enough for her. Carly seemed happy. She was still giving some last-second instructions to Parker.

"What if the rebels try to contact those two you took out in the gym? If they get no response over their radios, they might go over to check that out. They'll see that the hostages are gone and start a search. Won't they figure out that someone got in to help?"

"They'll probably figure that the hostages overcame the guards themselves."

"But—"

"Look, even if they do realize that the hostages are gone, they can't afford to send too many men after them. They need all the muscle they have to fight off the Russians. Ivan and the hostages we've given guns to should be able to handle a rebel or two."

"You're right. I was just…"

But he didn't look as if he was listening to her anymore. He was leaning toward the screen, narrowing his eyes at one of the grainy images.

"Damn. That is the dead-last thing we needed," he said.

Chapter Six

August 10, 21:30

Their situation was getting wilder by the minute. Parker stared at the screen. He shouldn't be surprised. Nothing that had to do with Kate had ever been easy.

He was only here to save her, but would she come willingly and speedily? Hell no. Always had to save the whole world and then some. *Easy* was not in the woman's vocabulary. Still, he could probably have handled it all, except for what—or who—appeared on the computer screen: Piotr Morovich.

He could have done without that complication. "What in hell is he doing now?" he hissed through his lips.

"Know him?" Kate asked.

"Yeah, and it gets worse. He knows me."

"Nice friends. Who is he?"

"A known anarchist and mercenary. His father was a Russian spy who was assassinated after defecting to France. He hates the Russian government and blames the French for not protecting his father well enough."

"Is he Tarkmezi?"

"Russian. From Kiev. But lately he's been hanging around with one of the Tarkmezi warlords."

"How do you know him?"

He stayed silent.

"I thought the Colonel said you could tell me things." Her emerald eyes flashed with impatience.

"On a need-to-know basis."

Her chest expanded as she drew a deep breath, getting ready to singe the hair off the top of his head. He braced himself for it.

"He is part of a group that has taken me hostage." She drew herself to full height, and even being several inches shorter than he was and much more slightly built, she did manage to look intimidating. "I'm stuck in an explosive-riddled building with him. My life is in danger. I *need* to know." The last words were said in a seriously pissed-off diplomat voice.

He drew an uneasy breath. She was right—to a point. And he was only too aware that this was the very issue he had lost her over in the past. "Piotr was looked into as a possible liaison."

"For what?"

He clamped his lips, aware that he had probably said too much already. He was walking a fine line here. But she was a smart one and, after a moment, put it all together on her own.

"You tried to recruit him to spy for the U.S.?" Her eyes widened.

"I evaluated him. A long time ago." Recruitment wasn't his territory. The SDDU had a handful of selected people for that—a task that had to be handled with the utmost delicacy. Since the group was top secret, before they approached anyone and revealed even the slightest information, they had to be a hundred percent sure the possible recruit would say yes.

"And?" She still had that dazed, Alice-down-the-rabbit-hole look on her face.

Made him want to kiss her senseless. Just about everything she did or said made him want to do things he could not, under any circumstance, do. And not all of them had to do with sex. Some had to do with turning back time. Good luck with that.

Or becoming the kind of man that she could love. *Don't go there, McCall.*

"Too unstable," he said, focusing on Piotr. An understatement, really. Piotr was one scary son of a bitch. But, God, what a relief it was to finally be able to level with Kate, at least about some of his work.

She pinched the bridge of her nose and squeezed her eyes shut for a second, visibly gathering herself before drawing herself straight and shaking off any momentary discouragement. "Great."

He kept an eye on the screen as Piotr moved along the long corridor, all alone. The man looked around then pulled a small package from his shirt.

No, no, no. Let it be a sardine sandwich. Parker's fingers tightened on the computer mouse, all of his attention focused on the man.

"What is he doing with the Tarkmezi rebels?" Kate was asking.

"That's the question of the hour, isn't it?" He watched the man step up onto an over-stuffed, antique armchair and pry off a vent cover, shove his package in there.

"What is that?"

He wasn't exactly sure, beyond that it couldn't have been anything good. And if his gut instinct was right, Piotr's little package could be something downright disastrous. "We'd better check it out."

He scrolled through the screens again, noting the rebel positions, how many of them there were at each spot, mentally mapping an escape route. The basement was completely closed off to the outside world, the roof occupied by Alpha troopers. He had to find a way out somewhere in between the two. And it wouldn't be easy. For one, all the windows had bars on them. Then there was the distinct chance that if he stuck as much as his head out, the Russians would shoot from the roof without stopping to ask questions.

They would need a distraction. He hefted the two TNT belts onto his shoulder as he stood, running all the possibilities through his mind one more time.

"There are two balconies," he told Kate as he headed for the door, weapon drawn. "The large one is on the second floor and it faces the front." All ornately carved stone. This was where the Russian flag flew. "The smaller one in the back is on the third floor and overlooks the yard." It was used for private dining for the ambassador and his visitors in the summer. "We'll try that one. We might be able to get over to the garage roof." Embassies had their own fleet of cars, a number of them bulletproof.

Since there were most likely no rebels in the garage or any of the outbuildings that belonged to the embassy, it was unlikely that the Alpha troops focused any serious manpower on those, after having swept them initially.

For a moment he considered getting Kate safely inside one of those bulletproof vehicles and sitting tight until the embassy was liberated. But he didn't much like that idea unless he had no other choice. Ideally, he wanted her far away from here by the time the serious fighting started.

They made their way over to the elevator shaft without trouble and he got them inside one more time. He was halfway up the ladder behind Kate when the Colonel called.

"The State Department is trying to work with the situation. The Russians know that our consul is in there with a bodyguard. All offers for help have been refused. They assured us of Ms. Hamilton's safety."

Which they both knew meant exactly squat.

"The media is camped outside the

building," the Colonel went on. "There's a live feed to most TV stations. Special news break and all that."

Great. That would make it that much harder to get out without drawing attention. He could not afford to have his picture pasted all over television as he was dangling from a rope down the side of the building with Kate Hamilton, the U.S. consul, in his arms.

"Piotr Morovich is here," he reported.

"For what?" The Colonel sounded as surprised as Parker had felt when he had spotted the man.

"He hates both the Russian government and the French. Beyond that, I have no idea. I guess this is why he came to Paris." They had figured he was here to put into place some weapons-exchange deal. Someone had passed on incomplete intel. On purpose? He needed to look into that once they got out of here.

"I'll check into it." Apparently the Colonel was thinking the same thing.

"Appreciate that, sir."

"Any change of status?"

"There are twenty-two rebels left as far as I could tell from the security cameras." Not all areas of the embassy had cameras, unfortunately. "I neutralized five so far. Had to be done, sir." He felt it necessary to defend his actions since the Colonel had asked him to get in and out with a minimum of interaction with anyone.

"Well done," the man said, not sounding upset by the news.

"Do we know who's leading the rebels?"

"Not yet. Wouldn't be Piotr, though."

Right. He wasn't Tarkmezi. Those fighters might have worked with him if he had something they needed, like information on the embassy, but they wouldn't follow a man not their own.

If he knew who the leader was, the most likely way to end the conflict quickly would be for him to locate the man and take him out. But with Kate by his side, his main goal was to avoid the rebels and not to go charging among them. More than anything, he wanted to keep her safe.

"How is Ms. Hamilton?" the Colonel asked. Didn't seem like he had taken offense over Kate hanging up on him earlier.

"Holding up well, sir. I'm going to try to get us out of the building and to the garage. I plan on checking on a package on the way out that Piotr put into the vent system. I'll report in if it's something important." And it was going to be, he knew that from the sick sensation in his stomach every time he thought of it.

They exchanged a few more words about enemy positions before hanging up.

"Are we going back into the vents again?" Kate asked with trepidation. But she looked ready to do it if he asked her. That was the kind of woman she was: strong, loyal and courageous.

He'd made a few whopper mistakes in his life, but he was beginning to think that letting her go might have been the biggest of them all. He struck that thought from his mind. He couldn't let himself sink into regret or the tempting fantasies of what could have been. They needed to get a move on.

"Not if we can help it. Keep your gas mask close at hand."

She nodded and resumed climbing—they had stopped for the phone call—and even in their dire situation, he couldn't help admiring her tempting lines and long-legged grace. A man would have to be dead not to notice. He saw something else, too. The tension in her body. He needed to distract her from the danger around them.

"Remember the orange duck at Meiwah?" he asked without meaning to. Meiwah, a high-end Washington, D.C., restaurant had been the venue for their first date. Obviously, he had food and sex on his brain. Not necessarily in that order. Hey, he was a guy; he wasn't going to apologize for that.

"Parker." Her voice was a soft plea.

She remembered it, all right, but didn't want to.

He'd walked her home after that first date, still deluding himself that he was doing it for the sake of his investigation. It had begun to rain.

Why don't you come in for a second? I'll dig up an umbrella for you. She looked mind-boggling in a white summer dress that had gotten just damp enough to stick to her curves.

Couldn't turn an invitation like that down, could he? A chance to look around her place—strictly in the interest of the case.

And then, *kaboom.*

To this day, he wasn't sure how they'd ended up kissing, how they'd ended up making love on the chaise lounge. It was pure insanity that first time, then the next and the next. He had waited for the breathless feeling in his chest to go away. It never did. They saw each other every day for the next two months—he was stateside for his investigation. The day he solved the State Department case, he proposed to her. Not that he had planned to. And he could barely believe when she had said yes.

He moved in with her the day after that, thinking it could work. Hey, there were a handful of guys in the SDDU who had families. Then, two days later, he got his marching orders to Taiwan for his next mission. For the next year or so, they barely saw each other.

He realized then that the relationship was probably torture for the both of them, but he would have married her in spite of his own judgment and the advice of his superior officer. Except that he had to lie to her the entire time, until she got sick of him and booted him right out the door.

And the hell of the thing was, he wanted her still, even now. Given half a chance, he would have found a way to make love to her in the dim elevator shaft, mark every inch of her body with his, sink himself deep into her soft heat. He wanted to hear her moan his name.

Sweat beaded on his upper lip by the time they reached the door to the third floor and she moved up on the ladder so he could get into position to open it. Better focus on the here and now if he didn't want to lose her. He opened the panels a crack as he'd done before, just enough to sneak a peek. The hallway was clear.

They got out and reached the turn in the corridor without trouble. But there was some muted noise up ahead. He used his phone camera to look around the corner, pushing it out low to the ground where he didn't think it would be noticed against the black marble tile. Five lounging rebels were doing nothing in particular up ahead, looking out the window. That portion of the corridor faced the courtyard. What were they looking at? Couldn't have been anything important, judging from their body language. Probably just passing time while their leader negotiated a deal.

They didn't look as though they were inclined to move anytime soon, which meant that he had to find another way to get around them. To reach the back balcony, he could have simply rounded the building with Kate. But he did want to take a look at what Piotr had left in the vent. That was crucial information he could pass along.

He motioned to the row of doors across the

hallway. Kate followed. None of them were open. And he couldn't make much noise. The rebels were just around the corner.

He got out his knife and the belt buckle from one of the TNT belts. The blade was too wide, the prong of the buckle not strong enough on its own.

"Flashlight," he mouthed to Kate.

She handed it to him and he took it apart, popped out the spring that kept the batteries pressed to where they needed to be. He bent it until it resembled the shape he required, then tried again. *Bingo*.

"We're gonna have to go back into the vent," he whispered when they were inside. Not knowing what in hell Piotr had put into the vent system, he really hated the idea.

He was torn between telling her to stay here in relative safety and taking her with him because he didn't want to take his eyes off her.

"Put your gas mask on," he said, deciding at last, pulling the stretch band of his own mask over his face. He made sure hers was on just as tight.

He opened the vent cover and pulled himself up first before helping her up behind him. He signaled to her to keep a fair distance. Didn't have to tell her to be quiet.

He could hear the guards talking, passed by them, reached the suspicious-looking package that he'd seen on the closed-circuit monitor before. Damn. He grabbed the capsule gingerly, signaling to Kate to back up.

He didn't talk until they were back in the room.

"What is it?" she whispered, pulling her mask off, rubbing the red marks the tight rubber had left on her face.

Good, that meant she'd had a tight seal. He didn't give her time to get comfortable. He tugged the mask right back over her face with his free hand.

"Some homemade chemical weapon." His voice sounded strange through the mask. He turned the capsule over. Surprisingly well put together. Whoever had made it knew what he was doing. He didn't think Piotr had this kind of expertise.

He took in the small sensor. "Remote release. It's fine for the moment, but the second someone pushes the control button somewhere in the building…" He gave her a meaningful look.

Kate drew back several steps, her hands on the mask now, pushing it tighter onto her face. "Do you think there are more?"

"I'd be willing to bet my 1969 Camaro on it." And he wasn't the type of guy who'd say those words lightly.

He looked at Kate and considered seriously, for the first time, that they might not make it out of here.

Chapter Seven

August 11, 04:31

"How can you stay so calm with a bomb in your hands?" Kate was hyperventilating behind her mask. Not just any bomb, a chemical-weapon bomb. *God.*

And he thought there was likely more.

"Practice," he said easily.

"You're nuts. Certifiable." And what did that say about her? She was trusting her life to him.

She thought of the other hostages, grateful that Parker had thought to provide them all with gas masks, grateful that they were in the basement and so were Elena and Katja. She didn't remember there being any vent openings down there. If anything happened up here, at least the hostages might yet be safe.

She hated the sight of Parker just holding

the wretched thing. If it were up to her, she would have been running the moment they'd figured out what it was.

"In how many ways are they planning to kill the hostages?" The rebels could easily have shot the embassy staff. She'd already thought the explosives were too much. And now the nerve gas? "Isn't this overkill?"

"Terrorists, in general, are not known for their restraint," he said dryly.

"Can you disable it?" She was half holding her breath, not a fun thing since the gas mask was an impediment to her breathing already.

He hesitated, then looked her square in the eye. "Not without tools."

Okay. He was being honest with her. That was what she wanted. What she had always wanted. But— *Oh God.* "What are you going to do?"

"Take it with us." He was putting it under his shirt already so his hands would remain free.

She caught a glimpse of tanned skin and flat abs. She had to be insane even to notice something like that at a moment like this.

And damn if he hadn't caught her looking. He arched a dark eyebrow. *Damn, damn and double damn.*

A hint of amusement underscored his voice when he spoke. "We can't leave it behind. We're going to have to find a way to deal with it before someone decides to set it off."

She so hoped he wasn't going to say that.

"That sounds like a good idea." Fear and anger at the unfairness of their situation bubbled up inside her, loosening something. "Why didn't I think of that?" It was hard to sound sarcastic with a mask on. "Oh, wait, I know. I must have thought that carrying around two TNT belts while sneaking among armed terrorists was dangerous enough." She was finally losing her cool, was aware of it, but couldn't do anything about it.

Morning was nearly here. She hadn't slept in two days. That and the constant danger had a way of making a girl cranky. And she wasn't even going to bring up her ex-fiancé's sudden and mysterious reappearance in her life. The kisses she was totally blocking. Indefinitely.

"I'm hoping to get it someplace where it'll do less damage than in the vents."

Okay, so there was some logic in that. The vent system was the worst possible place for a nasty-looking chemical weapon. "Like what?"

"A refrigerator or a freezer. Those doors are vacuum-sealed to keep the cold in. Not a perfect solution, but better than letting the airflow distribute all the poison through the whole building."

"The kitchen is on the first floor."

"I know. But they have diplomatic lunches on the back balcony when the weather is good. I'm betting there's at least a pantry somewhere nearby, and if we're lucky, there's a good-quality fridge."

AND THERE WAS. Unfortunately, they got very little time to spend with it, not even enough to grab some food. The rebels decided to go for a snack just a few minutes after Kate and Parker got there.

Six men were hanging out in the small indoor dining room in front of the balcony, coming and going from another room that was a pantry-slash-food-preparation station. They were eating and drinking, looking at the room's decorations and chatting as if they were on a field trip instead of a murderous mission. They had the flat-screen TV tuned to a soccer game.

Kate and Parker were hiding in a small closet behind a few dozen crates of soft drinks and some top-quality vodka. They'd been forced in there when the men came, and now they had no way out. There were no vent openings in here to crawl through.

Trapped.

She wiggled in the small space.

"Hang in there." Parker was watching her.

She focused on his eyes, which seemed to burn into hers even through the glass of the gas masks that were doing nothing to ease her sense of claustrophobia. She kept her gaze on him, trying to forget the lack of room, lack of air and the possibility that one of the rebels might get curious enough to look in there again.

The first one had nearly scared her to death. But apparently there were enough drinks available outside that he hadn't gotten excited by the sight that had greeted him in here. And, thank God, he hadn't looked too hard.

Her breath came in quick pants. She reached up to her mask. "Could we please take these off?"

He considered her for a long moment before he nodded. "Keep it at the ready."

She let it hang around her neck and took a full breath, then another.

The good thing about having no vent openings in the storage closet was that if Piotr what's-his-name activated the nerve gas and he had other capsules, the air wouldn't blow it in here. And, thank God, Parker had managed to put the capsule they'd had into the freezer in the other room before the rebels barged in, had even thought of submerging it in a bowl of water that would, she hoped, soon freeze into ice. He'd said it might mess with the remote control mechanism. She could only hope the rebels wouldn't find it as they foraged for food. They had no reason to look in there. They couldn't eat frozen food, anyway.

She rubbed the side of her face where the mask had left dents in her skin. Having her face covered so tightly added to her sense of unease. She wasn't an all-out claustrophobe, but she was very uncomfortable with small places, getting a rush of panic now and then that she fought with controlled breathing and sheer logic.

"You okay?" Parker whispered near her ear.

The TV wasn't loud enough to make out much except the roar of the crowd whenever the game took an exciting turn, but it drowned out the rebels' talking for the most part and Kate hoped it would mask whatever noise she and Parker might accidentally make in their hiding place.

They spoke in barely audible whispers, pressed against the back wall. Only a few inches separated them from each other. They were close enough for her to hear his even breathing, smell the familiar masculine scent of him.

What they said about scent being a potent trigger of memory was true. Memories flooded her. She fought back valiantly.

"I wonder how Elena and Katja are doing." She hadn't been able to get the two girls out of her head. Her thoughts cut back to them from time to time. They were tough little kids, hadn't been spoiled by life. But they were still kids. She worried about them.

"They're with people they know," Parker said reasonably.

But from the way he looked away from her, she could tell he was worried about them, too. "They didn't look like they knew that Ivan guy. Maybe he's new on the job," she said.

"I'm sure they don't know every single person who works here. But they probably know the kitchen staff. I bet they've eaten plenty of meals here at the embassy."

True. "And they would know Anna. She

is…was…their mother's secretary." She couldn't bear thinking of Tanya. If their circumstances were different and their meetings hadn't been limited to a few diplomatic luncheons, they could have been friends. She couldn't think of a nicer and more warmhearted person.

"Those poor kids lived in an orphanage for years. Then they're adopted by wonderful parents, and then— What do you think's going to happen to them?"

"They'll be saved. All of the hostages will be. They are in the most defendable location in the building. They have weapons. The rebels don't even know where they are. And the Russians will keep these bastards too busy to go looking for anything."

She sure hoped so. "I meant after that. Their parents are gone. Do you think they'll have to go back to the orphanage?"

"You can't help it, can you?"

"What?"

"You're always worrying about everyone," he said with a soft smile.

"*Worry* is the key word. Look what you're doing. You are risking your life for them." And had for countless others over the years, no doubt. "We didn't have a choice in being taken hostage. You waltzed in here all on your own, right into danger."

"They'll probably go to the rest of their family. I bet they have a boatload of aunts and uncles and cousins." He deftly steered the conversation back to the girls.

Of course they would have other family. Tanya had a large family and so did her husband. She hadn't thought of that. Good. That sounded good. Those children didn't need any more trauma.

"You didn't want children," she said without meaning to. The words just slipped out.

He looked at her in the dim space. The only light came from the inch-wide crack under the door.

"Just not right then. I figured we would have plenty of time. I wasn't in the position to take on that responsibility."

Considering the spot they were in at the moment, she could understand why he would have thought that. And this was what he did on a regular basis. It seemed almost incomprehensible. Who would do something like that?

Someone who cared deeply about others, who would risk his own life to keep others safe.

And she had thought him irresponsible

when he hadn't always called to let her know
he would be late.

"I assume there are other people on this
team of yours, whatever it is. Are any of the
others married? Nobody has any kids?"

He nodded yes with visible reluctance.

"And none of their wives know anything?"
She could sympathize with the women, with
what they must think, how they must feel.
She'd been there.

"Some do. Some are on the team, too."

That had to make it easier for them. Or
harder. They would know exactly what kind of
danger their husbands were in when they left
the house. If she'd known Parker was doing
this while they'd been living together, she
doubted she would have slept at night. She
had worried plenty back when she had thought
he was a foreign correspondent for Reuters.

She still felt betrayed and angry at the unfairness of life. Why couldn't she have fallen
in love with a regular guy instead of some
special commando soldier? But no, she
hadn't fallen in love with Parker, she could
see that with some clarity now. You needed
to know someone to fall in love with him. She
had fallen in love with the cover he presented.

This man was a lot more edgy, a lot harder,

a lot more dangerous. He did things that barely bore thinking about. He killed. She'd seen that firsthand.

And he protected her. With his life.

She filled her lungs, trying to stop that thought from worming its way to her heart.

He slowly ran a hand down her arm, and she closed her eyes.

That was the same. The way his touch affected her. Nothing changed there. And how unfair was that, on top of everything else?

He pulled her against him. "Try to get some sleep. There's nothing else we can do."

He wouldn't sleep. She knew that without him having to say it. He would guard them and listen to the rebels. He would wake her when they were gone.

She did need sleep; she was seriously dragging after two days of playing cloaks and daggers. But she didn't want to sleep against him. She wasn't nearly as impervious to him as she would have liked. She moved away.

He pulled her back again. "You are going to need your strength."

The heat of his body seeped into her, his scent, the feel of his arms around her. This time, she stayed where she was.

His chest rose and fell beneath her cheek.

Just like old times. She swallowed. There had been good times. She couldn't deny it. Fantastic times. She had been swimming in a surge of new love. What she'd *thought* was love. But there had been disappointments, too.

Or had she been too quick to judge? She wasn't going to go there. Hindsight might have been twenty-twenty, but it was also worthless.

He quietly moved the box next to him a few inches forward and maneuvered her deftly so she would end up on his lap, her head remaining on his chest and his arms around her.

They'd sat like this countless times before. It seemed they'd been always touching. Except when he had disappeared on "assignments."

But her mind was, at the moment, more inclined to drift over the good times. And then into dreams. Most were about danger, but Parker was there in every one of them, always on her side. Others were about naked bodies and breathtaking pleasure. Also with Parker in the starring role.

Her growling stomach woke her up. She felt disoriented in the small, dark space for a few moments, but registered Parker's protective presence and relaxed. She pressed a hand against her stomach.

"Sleep well?"

Well, but not nearly enough. She still felt exhausted. "I really needed that. Thanks."

The TV was still going outside. The game was over. Some woman was talking now. The news? She couldn't make out her words. She sounded excited and outraged, but then again news reporters always did.

She had no idea what time it was or how long she had slept. It had been forever since she'd eaten. Her body needed sustenance.

"Here." He must have heard her stomach growl, because he was handing her a can of soda.

Not much, but it had caffeine and enough sugar to keep her going a while longer.

She could feel the phone vibrate on Parker's belt. He took the call and she pressed her ear to the other side of it so she, too, could hear what was said. He didn't protest.

"VICTOR SERGEYEVICH is heading the rescue team," the Colonel said. "He was the KGB agent who assassinated Piotr's father. He's with the Alpha troops now, the leader of their counterterrorism team."

And Piotr probably knew that. He knew that if something as big as an embassy hostage crisis occurred, Victor would come. Piotr was here to draw and take out an old enemy.

"He has nerve gas," Parker whispered into the phone. "I retrieved one capsule. He probably has one for every floor." For all his faults, Piotr was a dependably efficient guy.

"Do you have gas masks?"

"Yes, sir."

"Good. I'll pass that information along. I'll tell them that our consul managed to get to a phone for a few seconds and contacted us with information. I've been holding back until now, not wanting to appear too suspicious. But at this stage we have enough to be of serious use. I'll tell them about the location of the hostages and ask for time before they attack. I want you out of there before that happens."

"We're near the rear balcony that over-looks the utility buildings and the garage. We'll be exiting through there most likely. I'd appreciate it if you could pass along a request to hold their fire if they see movement in that area. We're stuck near the exit point. Should be able to move within a few hours at the latest. Do you think you can gain us a couple of hours, sir?"

The Colonel didn't respond. Parker waited, pulled the phone from his ear to look at the display screen. Black. The battery was dead. They no longer had a way to communicate. The question was, how much had the Colonel heard of what he had said?

Chapter Eight

August 11, 15:06

Had he been on his own, he would have broken out and to hell with the consequences. He couldn't believe they'd wasted ten hours hiding in a stupid pantry when the clock was ticking. A growing tide of frustration simmered dangerously close to the surface. Every minute that passed brought them closer to disaster. But the rebels outside the door would not leave. They seemed to be hung up on the TV and the food.

At least he'd finally caught a few winks. Kate had insisted, and he trusted her to stand guard. They seemed safe in the storage closet and he needed to be at one hundred percent capacity when they finally broke out of here.

He had no idea how many rebels there were out there at this time, but by the voices alone he figured still about half a dozen, always shifting as some came and others left. Several times he had come close to kicking the door out and charging forward with guns blazing. But Kate was right behind him, no place to get cover in the closet. The plastic crates and soda bottles wouldn't stop any of the bullets the rebels sent his way. And he had no way of knowing if there might be one among them with a TNT belt who could set off his charge in the heat of the moment, taking out the whole room if not the whole floor.

What one considered "acceptable risk" sure had a way of getting reevaluated when you had the woman you cared about by your side.

"Parker?" She stood leaning against the opposite wall in the small space of the storage room, a foot or so away from him.

He already missed her body touching his. She had slept in his arms again. The memories of her sleeping in his arms on a regular basis seemed little more than a fantasy. A fantasy he would be only too glad to return to.

"I'm sorry," she whispered, her voice thick. "Back when—"

She stopped, and he leaned forward, waiting.

"I should have trusted you more," she finished.

His heart fumbled a beat with surprise. "We barely knew each other. And living with me is no picnic. Hey, I know that. You drew whatever conclusions you could, based on the information you had available."

Was she saying that maybe she regretted how things had gone down between the two of them?

"We still barely know each other," she pointed out as she watched him with those big emerald eyes that often haunted his dreams.

"At least now you know what I am." Maybe not the particulars, but she would have a fair idea of what he did for a living. And that probably wasn't a plus. She had seen him kill without hesitation. Two years ago, she had thought him uncommitted to their relationship and undependable. Chances were good that now she thought him a monster.

But she wouldn't sleep in a monster's arms. The thought gave him hope, more hope perhaps than he had the right to.

Her fingers fiddled with the bottom of her shirt. "You are so different from who I thought you were."

There it came. He held her gaze in the dim light, feeling as if a grand jury was about to pass judgment over him. He could have come up with a dozen excuses why he was the way he was, some pretty good ones among them. He didn't.

All he did was ask a single question. "Am I really?"

She closed her eyes for a second, drew a slow breath. "I suppose not that different," she conceded with an ironic little smile when she looked at him again. "I knew you were tough. It's just that you're tougher than I thought. And I knew that you were wild—" She paused. "But you are wilder than I could have ever imagined. I knew that you could be dangerous if someone threatened you."

He knew what she was thinking about. The small altercation down in Tampa when two lowlifes had tried to shove him out of the way to get to her purse. "I can be dangerous when *you* are threatened," he agreed, seeing absolutely nothing wrong with admitting that.

Another, longer pause followed.

"Thank you," she said. "For coming after me."

The tension in his chest eased a little, relief turning up the corner of his lips. "You bet."

Then he added, "Next time you want to see me and reminisce, you can always just call."

She took her turn to smile, but grew serious again after a moment. "Parker?" she whispered, quieter than ever.

He had to step even closer to hear her over the TV outside the door. "Yeah?"

They were about toe to toe.

She drew a deep breath that lifted her breasts, making his hands itch to touch them. "I missed you," she said.

His smile widened, and he reached for her, drew her into his arms, inhaled her scent and sank into the feeling of having her body flush against his. Fear never had the ability to weaken his knees, but now he realized that there existed a profound relief that could do just that. "I missed you, too."

They held each other, just processing those two short confessions, appreciating them.

"But I don't think we can just pick up where we left off," she said after several seconds.

Considering where they had left off, how angry they'd been, then no, definitely not. "We'll figure this out as we go."

Her lips nuzzled his neck, hesitant, as if she couldn't decide whether to go with the moment or pull away.

Neither his mind nor his body was in any sort of confusion over *his* preferred course of action. He held her tightly.

"But how far could it ever go? Until you disappeared again?" She pulled back enough so she could look him in the eyes.

"I have to disappear now and then. You understand what that's about now. But I'd always come back to you. Promise."

"Can you promise not to get hurt? That you'll be careful?"

That he could not do, not even for her, not even if he wanted to. His wasn't a careful type of occupation. "I can promise not to take unnecessary risks."

She pressed against him tightly the next second, holding him fiercely, as if she never wanted to let him go, and it made his heart sing. He ran his fingers up her arms, then neck, lifted her chin and brushed his lips over hers.

He hadn't meant to go much further than that. Okay, to be honest, he did hope to cop a feel or two. Holding her in his arms while she slept had riled his body. He tasted her bottom lip then the top one, tried hard not to think of what those lips could do to him. He was determined to remain in control.

Then she gave a little sigh that sent fire

skittering across his skin. And he swept inside her mouth and forgot all about his good intentions. She was sweet and hot and she was his, dammit. And he kissed her with enough passion to make sure she knew that.

And the good thing about Kate, one of the many that he had always appreciated about her, was that she always gave as good as she got. And then some. He nearly lifted out of his shoes when she gently sucked the tip of his tongue.

His hands that had rested on her waist now crept under her white top and the silk blouse under that, reveling in the feel of her soft, warm skin, spanning her narrow waist. She had lost weight in the past two years, but still wasn't what one would call skinny. Which titillated him on every level. He loved her curves, loved that lush, passionate body of hers. Could have sculpted it from memory.

Which, he thought thankfully, he had no need to rely on right now.

"Parker." She sighed his name in a voice saturated with passion.

Having his hands on her and hers on him, her soft lips beneath his, that unique scent of her and that voice of seduction surrounded him like a spell. There was no room to escape the onslaught of sensations, and he didn't want to. He wanted more of it, more of her. He let his palms slide over what they pined for and closed his fingers over her incredible breasts, resenting the thin fabric of her bra between him and her skin.

But then his thumb brushed against the front clasp and he smiled against her lips.

"Parker?" His name was whispered not on a voice of worry, but on a voice of need.

And he had need enough inside him to match hers, enough to drown in.

Her breasts were firm, the skin soft and smooth, her nipples hard against his palm. He groaned his satisfaction into her neck and kissed her there, the gentle slope that led toward her shoulder, the spot where he knew she was extra-sensitive.

He had no plans of seducing her completely or taking this too far. He just wanted her to remember. The trouble was, once he unbuttoned her shirt and sucked one dusty-rose nipple into his eager mouth, then the other, he seemed to forget all about his original intentions.

She let her head fall back and rest against the wall, arching her back, offering herself up to him. And he took it all, took everything he could, made her his feast.

He needed her. The thought made him straighten and crush her against him, and claim her lips again. He had always needed her, he'd just been too stubborn and full of himself to know it. He had thought he didn't need anyone, that the job was enough. And maybe there had been a time like that. But not after he'd met her.

He needed her. He had her for now. Out of that came the next logical thought: There was no way he was going to let her go again.

She might have something to say about that. The treacherous voice of doubt surfaced.

He would just have to convince her that she needed him. Judging from the glazed-over look in her eyes, he was on the right path.

He wanted her. That wasn't news. He had always wanted her, from the moment she had fumbled out of her car, all apologetic, asking him with big emerald eyes swimming in worry whether he was all right.

After they had split, he had hoped that eventually the wanting would stop, or would at least fade with time to a bearable level.

He'd been wrong. He knew that now. He was going to want her until the day he died.

He loved her. Now there was a thought to take the air out of his lungs. He loved her still. Maybe even more than before, although that hardly seemed possible. Then again, this time around he knew what it was like to lose her, so that added a whole other dimension.

"What is it?" She looked at him, her face flushed with passion, but concern leaping into her eyes. "Did you hear something?" she whispered.

He blinked, dazed but not confused. He knew without confusion what he wanted. But for that to happen, he had to get them out of here alive. With superhuman effort, he refastened her bra and smoothed down her shirt.

"I got carried away."

She watched him for a moment before offering a soft smile. "Yeah. Me, too. That hasn't changed, has it?"

He found it hard to focus on anything but her lips, which a few moments ago were deliciously under his. "Some things always stay the same. Forever."

It surprised him how good saying that word in connection to her felt.

She raised an eyebrow in a puzzled look

that said she was aware of the undercurrents in his mood, but couldn't quite make them out.

And this was not the time to explain.

Excited shouting outside drowned out the TV. Could be the most recent game was over. He could only hope and pray that the men would leave. They had cost him and Kate way too much time already.

"What time is it?" she asked. Her watch had been snatched when she'd been taken hostage at the beginning.

He glanced at his. "Just after five. In a couple of hours it'll be dark." And the Russian forces may take advantage of that and storm the building.

The noose was tightening.

Her stomach growled, and his answered, as if hunger was as contagious as yawning. He was used to going hungry. He'd been on assignments before where he'd had to fight his way out of the jungle with no food and little equipment, foraging as he went.

Not much to forage here. He handed her another soda—the only source of nourishment they had—and grabbed one for himself, too. He was swallowing a big gulp when the sound of breaking glass came from outside, making the drink go down the wrong way. He couldn't help coughing, but stifled it as much as he could. Gunfire. More coughing came from outside, too. People swearing savagely. His instincts had been honed in battle, and they didn't fail him now. He pressed Kate's gas mask to her face before he grabbed his own, securing it in place.

He couldn't make out her expression behind the mask, but her muscles were drawn tight, her body tense. He squeezed through the crates and listened to the gunfire that came less and less frequently. He cracked open the door. Smoke swirled. The men were fleeing. One still fired backward in the general direction of the balcony as he was running away. There were three on the floor, one still living, but gasping for air. He hadn't had his gas mask handy, apparently. The other two were dead or dying from multiple gunshot wounds. He assessed them as being past the ability to pose a threat.

"Let's go." He took one last glance toward the glass doors that led to the balcony. Broken now by the gas grenade the Russians had shot in.

Obviously, the Colonel had not heard when he'd told him that they would try to exit through the rear balcony. Or he had and had passed on the message, but the Alpha troops didn't care.

Their previous plan probably still firmly in her mind, Kate did step that way, crunching glass underfoot.

He shook his head and grabbed her arm to take her in the opposite direction, the way the rebels had fled the room. There could only be one reason why the Russians had cleared this place. But he had no time to explain.

In the end, he didn't have to. Outside, black-clad men rappelled down from above and swung onto the balcony. Except for the blazing guns, the scene looked like a ninja attack. They didn't stop to ask questions or demand identification. He couldn't blame them. He was wearing a rebel uniform that marked him as a clear target.

He shoved Kate out of the room ahead of him. "Go!" And took only one glance back. He meant to get a count on how many men were coming in, but the large-screen TV snagged his gaze. It showed the outside of the embassy. The cameras were showing a man's body being thrown from the other, larger balcony at the front of the building.

Parker didn't have time to linger. The Russians were shooting at him.

He ran down the hallway with Kate, ducked around the next hallway, then the next, opposite to where he heard boots thudding on marble, rebels coming to push the Russians out.

He went for the elevator doors as soon as they reached them, forced his way in and sealed Kate and himself inside.

"Are you hurt?" Kate hung on to the metal ladder for dear life with one hand, while trying to take the mask off with the other so she could talk more easily.

"Keep it on." His voice came out muffled. "I'm fine. You?" He looked her over carefully.

"I'm okay. Are they taking over the building?" Her voice sounded shaky and weak even beyond the mask's distortion.

"I don't think so." He'd only seen three Alpha troopers come down. "I think it's another distraction. The main force is probably trying to get in someplace else. Or they could have seen the rebel's leader through the window and figured if they took him out the rest would give up."

Not that he knew who the rebel's leader

was. He also had no idea what connection Piotr had to the guy. The operation was full of unknown elements. And what he did know, he really hated—like the explosive belts and Piotr's little capsules, and the fact that time was running out.

Gunshots sounded directly outside the elevator shaft. Just a few. Still didn't seem like this was a major battle. More like a small skirmish.

"The rebels found at least one of the hostages. Or, best-case scenario, one of them came up to look around." He told her what he'd seen on TV: he hadn't been able to make out the dead man's face, but he had recognized his clothes. He'd been part of the group in the gym with Kate.

Then came the sound of more shooting.

Russian forces were in the building. The rebels had started killing hostages again. And the whole place was booby-trapped. The situation inside the embassy was as volatile as possible.

"Where are we going next?" Kate asked.

He looked down, thinking of the hostages, wanting to help them. But his first responsibility was to Kate. A circle of light swooped by just above his head. He grabbed for the door.

"Out of here."

Looked like either the Alpha troops or the Vymple special forces had found the elevator shaft, as well, and had their own plans for it. He hadn't seen the Vymple team so far— he'd been wondering where they were and what they were up to.

SHE DIDN'T think the Russians had seen Parker and her. They didn't shoot. The elevator shaft was fairly dark and their faces were further darkened by their masks. Although she'd had a white top on at one point, it was now pretty much gray from the coal dust in the chute they had slid down and from all the dirt she'd crawled through in the vent ducts and their other hiding places.

Parker was working his magic on the door and got them out of there in a few seconds. Opening the door let light in and earned them a few shots from above, but they were already out of there too quickly to be in serious danger from that direction.

"Where can we go?"

Sounds of fighting came from the hallways around them. He motioned to the nearest vent covering. *Oh God.* She had so hoped that they wouldn't have to go back there. But the funny thing was, in the face of men with automatic weapons, having to crawl through a vent didn't seem nearly as scary as it had before.

He helped her up before coming in after her and closing them in.

"Which way?"

Gunfire sounded from their right. He went left. Didn't want to risk a stray bullet, she supposed. He moved fast, faster than before. With all the din outside, they didn't have to worry as much about making noise. She put what she had into it and kept up, tried to keep her breathing slow and controlled. Anyone who thought a tight vent tunnel was claustrophobic never tried being in one with a gas mask over her face. Under different circumstances she would have freaked out a dozen times by now, but Parker's calm presence and strength radiated over her somehow. She focused on him. He was going to get them out of this.

When they came to a section that led down to the floor below, Parker took it and she was glad for that. She was hoping they would somehow end up near the hostages and be able to help them. She wanted to make sure nothing happened to the kids.

He waited for her at the bottom. Wouldn't move forward.

"Are you stuck?"

"There's another capsule ahead."

She held her breath for a second. Would have held it indefinitely if she could.

"Your mask is on good and tight?"

She checked. "It worked before. It should work now, right?"

"Back there, they used some juiced-up tear gas. This is some sort of chemical weapon. A whole other ballpark." He moved forward slowly.

She couldn't see, but he must have reached the capsule because he stopped again.

"Is there a freezer on this floor, too?"

"I wouldn't think so. Let's find a window that looks out onto the street." He picked up the capsule.

They crawled straight for what seemed an eternity. Einstein had been right. Time was relative. Kate was fairly certain that having a chemical weapon ready to blow in your face stretched it.

"We are coming to a T in the duct," Parker said. And when she didn't respond, he added, "Could be we reached the outside wall." He moved up to the next vent cover and stopped there, looked out. He held up two fingers.

Which probably meant two rebels in the room below them that he could see from his vantage point. He motioned to her to move back and she did, then a little more and a little more as he asked for it.

She held her breath as he put the capsule down and pulled his gun, aimed carefully.

Someone shouted below them, then bullets came through the wall, three of them where she had been only moments before. Parker shot again. Twice. Everything fell silent down below.

"Okay. All clear." He was going down already, caught her in his arms when she crawled after him.

"Are you going to try to throw it out the window?" she asked, keeping her eyes averted from the bodies on the floor.

He nodded, but moved in the opposite direction instead, flicking the light off and plunging them into darkness.

"Just as soon not give them a target. I'm sure there are sharpshooters up front." He crept to the window and looked out, then stepped aside and pressed himself to the wall next to it, opening the window with one hand.

"What about the people on the street?" she asked.

"I'm sure the French have the street secured by now. Probably the whole block."

Ornate bars bolted to the walls made it impossible for a person to pass through them. But the capsule would fit.

Parker moved back and took his camouflage shirt off, wrapped the capsule in it, and was left wearing a dark-gray undershirt that stretched over his flat abs and his impressive biceps.

"I don't want this thing to break and go off," he said. "I'm aiming for the grassy patch on the traffic island. The French terror response units out there will have someone with the right tools to disable the damned thing."

He drew the capsule above his head with his right arm, swung a couple of times like a national league pitcher. And then he went for it.

The capsule sailed through the bars without trouble. Floodlights hit the window the next second. Kate squinted against the glaring light, backing away from the window as far as possible. But not before she caught sight of Parker's arm, heavily bleeding.

"When did you get shot?" She moved toward him instinctively.

Not here. No gunfire came from outside, just the sweeping floodlights.

"Back into the vent. Up, up, up." Parker was pushing her in front of him, not taking his chances.

"DID YOU get hit in the elevator shaft?" Kate's voice was thick with concern.

For him. Maybe there was hope for the two of them yet. Parker closed the vent cover behind him, making sure to have it flush against the wall. "Grazed."

He didn't want to give her one more thing to worry about.

"You can't know that. We'll have to stop somewhere and look."

"Believe me, a graze on the skin feels different enough from a shot through flesh and bone to know." He could recall several instances clearly. "You can look at it to your heart's content when we get out of here. But I think we should get going now."

"You've been shot before?" She began crawling forward, but was moving with clear reluctance.

He followed and kept quiet. He was good at blocking pain, a learned skill most people who were in his line of work eventually developed. You couldn't let pain distract you on a mission.

"Parker?" Her voice was a whisper, but a sharp whisper. She wasn't going to let this go.

"The scar on my lower back."

"Your dog bite?"

"They're more like shrapnel holes. I'm missing a kidney there."

"Oh my God." She sounded genuinely horrified.

"Not that bad. I had a spare." He made light of it, but the truth was the injury had very nearly cost him his life. If it hadn't been for Jake Kipper's quick thinking and expert care, it would have. Jake, who was dead now, along with the wife he had loved more than life itself.

The gunfire was receding in the distance.

"Do you think the rebels beat the Russians back?" she asked.

"I doubt it. Unless that is what the Russians want them to think."

"I expected a bigger attack."

"There'll be one. Count on it. Only three Alpha troopers rappelled into the dining room through the balcony. Could be they only came in to place some hidden cameras so they can figure out how to structure the main attack."

"How soon do you think that'll come?"

"I can't remember any cases when the Russians let a hostage situation go beyond seventy-two hours. After that, it gets hairy for the hostages without food and water and medical care." And it got dicey for the Russian authorities, who didn't like to appear as though they didn't have everything under control.

She reached a point in the duct where she could go down one more floor and did, making a slight noise that he didn't think would be noticed under the circumstances. The rebels would be focused on the intruding force, distracted by intermittent gunfire.

He slid down behind her, holding his arms out to control his fall. She had already moved forward in the duct to make room.

"We're on the ground floor now. West corner of the building," he told her.

"Can we get out through here?"

"The front entrance is probably heavily secured by the rebels. The back doors to the courtyard probably have a half dozen high powered rifles aimed at them."

"Where can we go, then?" she asked.

He could hear the desperation and the

panic in her voice, but to her credit she didn't show any of that in her actions. "Back to the basement."

Her shoulders relaxed. Probably from the thought of being back with the girls again. "Good. We can stay put with the hostages until the Alpha Team or whatever takes the rebels out."

"Or not. I think it's time to get out of this place."

"But you said there was no way out of the basement." She glanced back at him.

He grinned under his gas mask and lifted his shoulder to jiggle the belts of TNT. "We are about to make one."

Kate picked up speed. Looked like she was fully behind the idea.

"Keep an eye out for funny-looking capsules," he said. There were still a number of things that could go disastrously wrong. But this was the only one he wanted to bring to her attention. The others they could do nothing about so there was no sense in wasting energy worrying over them.

"You think there's more?" Her voice was hesitant, but she didn't slow.

"So far we picked up one on the third floor and one on the second floor. Piotr couldn't have smuggled in many more without his buddies seeing it."

"You don't think the other rebels know about the capsules?"

"I don't think so. Remember how he kept looking over his shoulder while we watched him place the first capsule on the security video? I think this is his private agenda. He managed to lure his archenemy into this building. He's going to take the guy out no matter what it takes. Even if it means killing the rest of the rebels or killing himself, too, in the process. Keep your mask on and be prepared for anything."

They crawled in silence for a while before she asked, "How long has it been since the rebels took over?" Then she shook her head and gave a small groan. "It's bad enough I lose all sense of directions in the ducts. Now I'm losing my sense of time."

"Happens when you don't get enough sleep. And don't get enough outside light. And when you're under attack," he added after a moment. "Combat time doesn't feel like real time. It takes a while to get used to it."

Amazing that she had held up as well as she had, that she wasn't sobbing in some corner yet, hadn't given up. She was a strong woman, something he had always loved and respected about her. He glanced at his watch. "Two and a half days."

"What about it?"

He was getting used to the raspy way her voice sounded through the mask. It didn't remove any of the sexiness.

"That's how long we've been here," he said. "Two and a half days." And he was frustrated as hell that he hadn't been able to get her to safety in all that time.

"That can't be right," she said hesitantly.

"Seems half as long, doesn't it? Time flies when you're fighting for your life."

"The fighting picked up," she said.

"The Russians are about to start a full-out attack."

"How long do we have?"

"A couple of hours at best."

If they were lucky. If they weren't, they could have a lot less than that.

But even if they did reach the basement, there was no guarantee that the hostages were still there, that any of them were still alive. He had played down the scene he had caught on TV—that man being thrown from the balcony. But he was only too aware of the implications.

They couldn't discount the chance that the rebels had taken the basement. And even if they hadn't, he had little structural information on the building. The Colonel had been more concerned with the layout when he was passing information through the phone. There was a chance that they couldn't, in fact, blow their way out.

Which meant they'd be trapped.

Chapter Nine

They had wasted hours, time they didn't have, because the ducts didn't always follow the hallways, didn't always connect.

But they were finally in the home stretch, passing by the kitchen. Even if he didn't know from the quick but detailed description of the building's layout the Colonel had given him, the smell of fried oil and spices would have given it away.

Neither of them had eaten a decent meal for what seemed like forever. His stomach was so resigned to the lack of food, it had even given up growling. Kate was definitely getting slower.

And he feared that the worst of the fighting was yet to come.

"I'm so hungry my knees are shaking,"

she said, confirming that she needed nourishment to face what they had to on their way out.

And that was probably how all the hostages felt.

He figured they could get in and out of the kitchen in under two minutes. "Let's see if we can grab something. I'll go first."

Kate crawled past the vent hole to make room for him. He peered out, noted the deserted kitchen that looked as if a family of baboons had looted it, food wrappers and boxes tossed all over the place. He hoped the scavenging rebels had left at least a few bites of something edible behind.

He couldn't see anyone. Wouldn't have minded checking out the wall directly under him that he couldn't see from his current position, but his cell-phone camera didn't work with a dead battery.

He waited and listened. No sound of movement or breathing came from down below. The gunfire he heard was in the distance. Sounded as though the rebels were fighting on one of the higher floors.

He pushed out the vent cover, turned it and pulled it in so it wouldn't crash to the floor and attract attention. The kitchen doors were open. There could be anyone out there in the hallway, guarding this section of the building.

"Give me a minute to look around," he said over his shoulder and stuck his head out little by little, his handgun at the ready.

A gloved hand came up from below and clamped around his neck the next second, pulling him until he crashed headlong onto the tile floor. The fall rattled his brain, the hand nearly crushing his windpipe.

Damn. Anger flooded him and a split second of fear, not for himself, but for Kate. If he stupidly let himself be killed, who was going to get her out?

He struggled for air behind the gas mask, fighting off the man as best he could. He couldn't get the gun between them, his hands blocked by the attacker's, their bodies twisted together as they rolled on the kitchen floor, groping for hold and leverage like wrestlers. The other guy had on a gas mask, too, his face obstructed.

The man was strong. Heavy, too, and un- affected by injury and hunger. He had to get Kate out of here.

"Go!" he yelled, his bruised windpipe hurting from the effort, hoping she would heed him, and not go into her typical leave-no-man-behind routine. She would have made a hell of a soldier. She was a hell of a woman.

"Get out of here," he ordered again in his best superior-officer tone that no man had ever dared refuse. Whoever the attacker was, he must have heard him talking to Kate before he'd stuck his head out of the vent, so the guy would already know Parker wasn't alone. Would already know Kate's position. He was giving no new information away.

He finally got his gun where he wanted it as they twisted, but so did the other guy. He heaved back. Both guns discharged at the same time, neither hitting its aim, but one leaving a hole high in the wall. Right about where the ducts were.

Parker swore, his breath hitching. "Kate?" he asked without daring to take his eyes off the enemy. They rolled again.

No answer came.

He chanced a glance that way. Couldn't see anything.

Dammit.

The guy went for Parker's gas mask with his free hand just as Parker grabbed for his, and they managed to unmask each other at the same time.

"Piotr?"

They both stilled for a split second. The man seemed surprised to see Parker, but got over it fast and rolled him. He was heavier by a good fifty pounds, and strong as the proverbial Russian bear. Working out had always been his religion. That was how Parker had first gotten to him—through his gym and his steroids supplier.

They rolled on the floor, among the garbage the foraging rebels had left strewn all over the place, until they banged into the kitchen island, sending pots and pans rattling inside.

"Working for the Kremlin now?" Piotr spat at him, but missed.

The man wasn't thinking clearly. But as soon as he had time to mull things over, he would know that Parker wouldn't switch sides, that he was still connected to the U.S. government. Piotr was a serious liability. To Parker personally, to his cover, to his team, to the current operation and operations to come. Piotr wouldn't sit on a piece of juicy information like this for long.

Parker heaved and got the upper hand, rolling them against a table. Plastic storage boxes bounced to the floor. He brought his right hand between them slowly, millimeter by millimeter, grunting along with Piotr. He almost had the guy when a bullet whizzed by him and he had to roll again, letting go of the man, giving up the gained ground.

The Alpha trooper dressed entirely in black who'd appeared out of nowhere kept on shooting at them. To him, the scene must have looked like two rebels had gone fist to fist over something, possibly food. He didn't give them time for explanations, nor could Parker have explained who he was and what he was doing here, even if the chance presented itself. He fired back while keeping on the move, working to get out of the open.

Then fire opened from another point. High up on the wall. *Kate.*

Which meant the round that Piotr had fired into the wall hadn't hurt her, or at least not too badly. Parker breathed a little easier. But damn it all, she wasn't supposed to be here. And she sure as hell wasn't supposed to engage the enemy.

She had surprised the Alpha trooper and distracted him long enough for Parker to roll behind a counter as near to Kate as he could get. He sprayed the room with bullets the next second, providing her with cover until she could crawl farther into the duct where she couldn't get hit. She had gotten him out of a tight spot, but now that he had everything under control, she needed to draw back and remove herself from harm's way. He kept up the rapid fire.

And swore when she tumbled out of the vent opening head-first, rolled across the floor and was by his side the next second. All he could do was stare. Even his finger stopped on the trigger. But it didn't seem the other two men cared. They used the lull to go after each other.

He scanned the room, noticed the small Russian army issue rucksack by the wall. Probably Piotr's. Most likely, he'd been in here to put another capsule in the very vent opening Parker had popped out of. What were the chances the remote control device was in the bag and not with Piotr?

At least the man was going nowhere for the moment. The Alpha guy had him pinned.

Parker rested his weapon and signaled to Kate to do the same with hers. "Let them kill each other." He looked toward his mask that lay in the middle of the kitchen where Piotr had ripped it off.

He should get that back before the bastard decided to set his knapsack off.

Kate had pulled her mask off at one point. He reached out and pulled it back into place, caressing what little skin it left bare with the back of a finger.

She held his gaze through the glass. "Who are they?"

"Piotr put out the capsules. The Alpha guy must be Victor, the man he'd been hunting most of his life." He'd already told Kate some of the story when the Colonel had given him the information.

Bullets flew in the air as the two men sparred. Parker drew Kate next to him to protect her with his body, kept his own weapon ready. The air was filled with the acrid smell of discharged weapons and plaster dust from the bullets that had missed their targets.

"How long are they going to keep at this?" she asked above the din.

"Until one of them is dead." He was pretty sure about that. He was hoping it'd be Piotr—before he had a chance to release whatever it was that he'd put in the capsules. Probably nerve gas. Hard to tell just by looking. Parker measured the distance to his gas mask.

Too far.

The men ran out of bullets at about the same time. There was a moment of silence, then Piotr roared. They went at each other like charging buffalo. Piotr was a big man, bigger than the other guy, but that one was solid muscle. The floor practically shook from their collision.

Both were bleeding, Parker registered, but neither was wounded fatally.

He could have finished them now, was ready to do it at a moment's notice. But something held him back. The men were no danger to Kate and him just now, their attention focused on each other as they were locked in a fight to the death.

Little by little, Piotr gained the upper hand. He didn't waste the momentary advantage. He put his considerable weight into it and choked the life out of his opponent with his bare hands, held the man down until he went limp.

"Okay." Parker rose, keeping his gun at him. "Now hand over the remote. I know about your capsules. You got what you wanted. Game over."

Piotr turned slowly, as if he'd forgotten in the haze of his murderous rage that anyone else was in there. He stood, took another look at the body at his feet, then pulled a small plastic device out of his pocket.

For a moment, Parker thought he *would* hand it over. Then Piotr reached for the gas mask hanging around his neck. He didn't seem inclined to listen to reason. Or maybe he was smart enough to know that whatever happened, Parker was never going to let him walk out of here.

Parker fired at the man's wrist. He wanted to make sure that a reflex twitch wouldn't push that button as it might have if he'd gone for the heart. He hit his aim as he'd known he would, and lurched for the remote that flew out of Piotr's destroyed hand, expecting the guy to do the same.

But Piotr made a run for the door, and by the time Parker came up with the remote, the man was gone from the kitchen, leaving a trail of blood behind him.

"Put that rucksack in the freezer," he told Kate. Thank God they were in the kitchen. He grabbed his gas mask. "Then get back into the duct and stay there until I come back." He sprinted after the man without looking back.

He hated to leave her alone, even if for a

moment. But he couldn't let Piotr go and he could move faster without having to watch out for Kate.

KATE SHOVED the rucksack into the freezer, into a drawer on top that said Rapid Freeze. Then she ran after the men.

They charged into the staircase. She followed them, and could hear the door open then slam shut one flight down. The main level. She wasn't sure where they would come out. The resplendent lobby? Or these could be backstairs leading someplace else entirely. The door opened again. A hail of bullets came before it slammed shut this time.

"Parker?"

Sounds of energetic swearing came from below. Then she turned on the landing and could see him, the point of his knife in the lock as he tried to turn it.

"They locked us out?"

"I'm trying to lock *them* out. What are you doing here? Can't you follow the simplest order?" He gave her that hard, military-intimidation stare that seemed to be the new Parker's default expression. "Half the rebel force is out there, dammit."

A round of shots sounded the next second, proving his claim. Thankfully the door was bulletproof. They had a staircase like this at the U.S. embassy, as well, their "safe place" where all employees were expected to gather in case of an attack until they could be rescued. It was fire- and bulletproof with a vent that pumped in fresh air, no windows, designed to be able to withstand a lot if terrorists or rioters attacked the building.

Unfortunately, this staircase didn't go below the main level; it ended where Parker stood. They had to go back up and find another way to the basement to see if they could help the hostages and bust their way out of here with the explosives they had. She was glad Parker had had the presence of mind to arm those people.

He was running up the stairs, while behind him the rebels were pounding on the door, trying to break it down.

When they were up and out in the hallway again, Parker took the lead, heading back toward the kitchen. They rushed through, keeping an eye out for food, though not seeing any until Parker came across a bag of rolls and biscuits on a high shelf and they stuffed those into their pockets, a few stale croissants into their shirts.

When the food was safely tucked away, Kate headed toward the vent opening, but Parker said, "Piotr saw us coming out of there. They'll be looking for us in the ducts." He was searching again, opening pantry doors.

"What are you looking for?"

"Service elevator. According to the Colonel, the kitchen was moved to this floor from the ground floor recently. Since it no longer has a street-level entry for deliveries, they have to get stuff up here somehow. I doubt they bring sacks of potatoes through the marble grand foyer to the main elevator banks."

Made sense. She went to help. The first door she opened led to cold storage. The second revealed a dead-end hallway. And stainless-steel elevator doors. "Bingo."

She didn't expect much to happen, but she pushed the button anyway and was surprised when it lit up. "It works?"

Parker was next to her already. "The rebels might not know about it. They might have older information on the building, without the new kitchen."

Maybe his Colonel did, too. Otherwise, wouldn't he have given Parker the location of the service elevator? She didn't have much time to worry about that as the doors opened.

She grabbed a croissant out of her shirt and shoved nearly half of it into her mouth. She was so hungry it was a miracle her brain still functioned.

Parker smiled at her and did the same. "Should have gone back to the duct until I came for you." He couldn't seem to be able to help himself from lecturing, but did it mildly.

"Could have stayed with me."

"I need the guy."

He explained to her how serious a security risk Piotr was. Piotr knew him. Could blow his cover, which would jeopardize his team and future missions.

"Why didn't you shoot him in the kitchen while you had the chance?"

He made a strange face, his cheeks puffing out with food. He looked unbearably cute in a very macho and dangerous way. God, he was the handsomest man she had ever seen. The only man who could turn her on with a look in the middle of a hostage crisis. She was one sick puppy. Or— No, she wasn't going to consider that. She was not, under any circumstances, going to fall back in love with Parker McCall.

"The guy Piotr took out, Victor Sergeyevich, was responsible for his father's death," he said, then fell silent.

"So you gave him a chance to get justice for that?"

He shrugged.

"But you *are* going to kill him, right? I mean, that's the goal."

"I have to."

She couldn't say she completely understood the workings of Parker's mind. He was operating under his own sense of justice at the moment it seemed. "Look, his father— When my father—"

He looked away from her, as if expecting some sort of judgment.

"Hey." She put a hand on his shoulder. "Piotr is the bad guy here."

He looked up with a surge of hope in his eyes. The breath caught in her throat. She swallowed the last bite of food. So did he. He leaned forward. She held her breath. Something dinged.

The service elevator was so slow it took a full minute to go down one floor, but they were finally there.

"Stand aside." Parker pulled back and stepped in front of her with his gun drawn. The doors opened. Bullets flew in.

Okay, so the rebels did know about the elevator. They hadn't disabled it for a reason. Maybe they needed it for a part of their plan.

Parker was shooting back, and she did, too, as best as she could from behind him. He was leaning on the Close-Door button with his free hand until, after an eternity, the thick metal doors slid together again.

"I was afraid of this," he said, his mouth set in a grim line.

"Are we trapped?" She was breathing hard, her heart going a mile a minute.

He looked up. "Not quite." Then he was reaching up, dismantling the ceiling. "Keep pushing the button so they can't open the door."

And they were trying. She could hear them. She fused her index finger to the button while Parker worked on getting them out of there. He had the decorative panel off in seconds revealing a small door. She'd only seen stuff like this in movies.

He jumped for the ledge and pulled up. The next second, all she could see were his dangling feet. Then he was gone.

"Push the button for the kitchen." He

reached back down for her. "Wish the damn thing went higher."

So did she. Whatever he had in mind, they only had about a minute before the elevator reached the kitchen, opened, and the rebels who would run up the stairs to meet it realized Kate and Parker weren't inside. It wouldn't take them long to figure out that they were up on top. She didn't see what Parker's plan was, but there was no time to question his judgment. She pushed the number one button, then reached for his hand and let him pull her up, trusting herself to him.

The elevator started with a shudder and some scraping sounds.

"Come on, we're getting off," he said.

"Here?" she asked, bewildered.

But he was already stepping over to a ledge of bunched wires on the side. There was enough room in the shaft for him to fit by the elevator if he flattened himself against the wall.

It looked dangerous. She peered down as the elevator inched past him, covering him up to the knees, then up to the waist.

"Come on."

She reached for a bundle of wires and

stepped over quickly, holding her breath until she found sure purchase with her feet and both hands, sucking her stomach in and cursing her breasts, which stuck out. But she made it. Barely.

Deep breath. The elevator was rising, and she found it harder and harder to stay still as the elevator neared her head. She felt trapped, about to be crushed. Not that being spread on the wall was her only worry.

"Aren't we going to get electrocuted?"

"Only if you touch the wrong thing," he said, perfectly calm.

"What's the wrong thing?" She had to yell to be heard. She might have yelled anyway. In fact, she decidedly felt like screaming.

"You'll know when you touch it," he said.

She felt the urge to escape, but panic kept her pressed to the spot. There was an equally strong urge to strangle Parker at the earliest opportunity. Which, after a moment, she did recognize as unreasonable. He hadn't gotten her into this situation.

Well, he did get her into *this* situation, but not the whole embassy-hostage-crisis deal. He'd come to save her. He just didn't realize that she wasn't a professional and that likely he was going to kill her in the process.

For a few moments she was completely blocked in by the elevator, the heavy machinery moving inches from her ears like some horrific creature, ready to grind her up. It pushed the air around, giving her the eerie feeling that the great beast was breathing down her neck.

"Parker..." she said in a weak voice, not expecting him to hear her over the noise. But his warm hand closed around her calf and anchored her, both to the wall and to reality. So maybe she could wait a little longer before she strangled the man.

Then the elevator passed by her, and Parker tugged. She wasn't about to move.

"Let's go."

Okay. But only because she couldn't stay here forever. She tried desperately to decide which wires were the wrong ones so as not to touch them.

They lowered themselves to the bottom of the shaft about fifteen feet below, careful not to step on anything that looked as if it might give them a nasty shock. The closed doors that led out of there were about waist high.

They listened first. No noise came from outside. The rebels had probably run up to meet the elevator in the kitchen.

Parker did something to the wiring on what looked like a maintenance panel, then jammed his knife in the slim slot where the doors met and pried them apart far enough so his fingers would fit in there. Nobody started shooting outside. Encouraging. After another moment, he was able to pull the doors open enough for them to fit through. He went first, then helped her out.

"Where are we?" she asked.

"In a back hallway near the embassy's courtyard."

There were no windows, only a steel-reinforced door. He tried that. Locked.

He glanced at the TNT belts on his shoulder, then said, "The Russians probably have all the exits covered. Let's get down to the basement and check on the hostages. We can always try this if we can't get out through there."

"Which way?" She'd gotten turned around again, enough so she couldn't remember where the basement door was. She had a deplorable sense of direction, something he used to tease her about back in the day.

He took off as sure as an arrow. She rushed after him, keeping her gun at the ready. They moved as fast as possible. It wouldn't take long for the rebels to figure out what had happened and come back down to look for them here. This was the only other exit from the elevator shaft.

They were in the back areas of the embassy, nowhere near the marble-tiled grand foyer and its twenty-foot-high ceiling. The hallways were narrow and the flooring the same heavy-duty tile usually used in hospitals. When they finally reached the basement door, they flattened themselves to the wall outside it, one on each side, stopping to listen.

No sounds came from downstairs. It could have been that the door was heavy enough to block any sound.

Parker reached out and turned the knob silently. It gave. That didn't bode well. Ivan was supposed to have barricaded the door.

She thought of Elena and Katja, her heart beating in her throat.

Parker looked at her.

"I shouldn't have let them go," she mouthed the words miserably.

He cocked his head and raised his eyebrows.

Okay, fine, so they'd been in a hairy spot or two since she'd sent the girls to what she'd thought was a safe place. So maybe they wouldn't have been better off with her. She was going to reserve judgment until she found them.

Parker went first and after a moment or two she followed.

They took the stairs one step at a time, careful not to make noise. Nobody was talking below, but there were some odd sounds and clothes rustling, so they knew there were people down there.

Had to be the hostages. *Alive.* She relaxed marginally. The rebels wouldn't just be hanging out down here when there was fighting going on upstairs. Instinct pushed her to rush forward, but common sense held her back.

Then Parker stopped and held up a hand, staring intently at something out of her range of vision. She stayed motionless for a minute, then took the few steps that separated them, using extra care not to make even the slightest noise.

A pair of feet came into sight first, then the torso of a man, lying on the ground at an uncomfortable angle, motionless. Then she could see the top of the chest, covered in blood, and knew, even before she could see the cook's vacantly staring eyes, that he was dead.

PARKER MOVED lower on the stairs, signaling to Kate to stay where she was, hoping this time she would listen. "Be careful," he mouthed, a last admonition before turning his full attention to what waited ahead.

Something had gone terribly wrong down there. The tension was so thick in the air he could smell it over the musty scent of the old brick walls that drew cold moisture from the ground.

He'd had visual of one body, but sensed more people down here very much alive. Whether hostages or rebels, he didn't know. They were to the left, farther ahead where he wouldn't be able to see them until he reached the bottom of the stairs, stepped out and would be without cover. He moved inch by inch, registering and evaluating each and every sound, letting the cool of the basement surround him and revive him a little. The elevator shaft had been hellishly hot.

He stole down another step. Another body came into view. Black pants, white coat, same as the first. Another one of the kitchen staff. His stomach tightened.

When Kate and he had been down here, there'd been crates of salt to his left. But he couldn't count on them still being there. If they weren't, then with the next move he would be out in the open.

He didn't hesitate at the last step, just went around the corner.

The crates were there.

The surviving hostages, only eight, sat twenty or so feet from him on the floor, tied together and gagged this time. His gaze went to the two little girls first, who were pressed up against a young woman. He put a finger to his mouth lest somebody made some noise and betrayed him. The woman signaled something with her eyes to the kids. They stayed quiet. She fixed him with an urgent look and glanced toward the back of the basement, then at the people next to her.

He got it. He'd figured there were some rebels down here.

He quickly skimmed the rest of the hostages, taking in the red-rimmed eyes and exhausted faces, registering that Ivan was among them. He had expected him to hold up better and protect the rest.

He stepped farther out, not exactly into the open, but away from the cover of the salt crates, keeping his focus on the dark places in the shadows, looking for the enemy. A man or two, no more. Just enough to keep an eye on the hostages. The rebels couldn't spare more when a desperate battle was raging above.

He saw movement in a maze of boxes, shot at the shadow of a man and was shot back at. On instinct, he rushed forward, keeping low to the ground, putting himself between the rebel soldier and the hostages. Then a blunt force hit his left shoulder from behind, as if he'd been smacked by a football at top speed.

But this wasn't a varsity game, and he knew what being shot felt like.

This was it.

Chapter Ten

August 12, 00:50

Kate stood back, higher up the stairs, waiting for Parker's go-ahead signal. But instead, when he got to the bottom, he stepped around the wall and she couldn't see him. She couldn't see anyone. She had no idea what was going on when the first shot exploded.

Her brain was screaming to get out of there. Her heart pushed her forward, toward Parker.

More shots came. She held her gun at the ready as she carefully crept down the stairs, pressed against the wall, going sideways so she would present as small a target as possible if someone came running up. Parker had told her to do that. He'd given her a dozen small tips for staying alive while they'd been stuck in various places in the last three days.

Not that he followed his own advice. Whenever they were together and heading into trouble, he always went first to block as much of her as possible.

She listened, jittery enough to jump out of her skin at the next shot. And another, and another. Still nobody had said a word down there. She could smell her own fear in the air, her mouth as dry as the dusty vent ducts had been. She was no soldier. Her index finger twitched on the gun's trigger. *Not good.* What in hell did she think she was doing here?

Saving Parker.

She steadied her hands and eased down another step. She saw the dead bodies first. Hostages. Her heart clutched. She moved lower, and then she saw him in the crossfire, ducking bullets as best he could with no cover. Her heart tripped when she spotted the blood on his shoulder. A man sitting among the hostages was shooting at him from one side. Ivan? What— Another took potshots from behind the solid cover of a stone wall in the far corner.

She aimed at Ivan. His Russian dress uniform—obviously it had been a cover— stood out. He was sitting among the hostages, making it hard for Parker to fire back as men and women scrambled around, some shouting, trying to get out of harm's way unsuccessfully, frustrated by the ropes that bound them. She spotted the children—*alive,* thank God, still unharmed. They were crying, but their voices were lost in the cacophony of the attack.

Parker ducked behind some boxes finally, not that they offered any protection. The bullets Ivan shot at him sliced straight through the cardboard. And he was still open to the attacker on his other side. He was focusing on holding that man back, reluctant to shoot toward the hostages.

The pop and bang of bullets echoed in the basement. At any moment the rebels could reach them, following the sounds of a gunfight. But before that happened, there was a chance that the Russians could gas the building, or one of the human-bomb rebels could blow it or if Piotr had another capsule, he could set that off.

Moving, trying anything seemed futile against such overwhelming odds. Part of her wanted to fall to the floor and curl up where she was, and hope that when the end came, it would be quick. Her mind was numb with the possibilities of death.

She couldn't afford numb. The problem manager in her mind took over.

Parker needed her help. The girls needed her, and so did the other hostages. She drew a deep breath and cleared her thoughts as best she could, resolving to work on the disasters that threatened them one at a time. First, the one right in front of her.

She gripped her gun. Nobody had noticed her yet in the mad fight. She had a different view of Ivan than Parker, a better angle. She adjusted the gun's sight until she had the man's head in the crosshairs. When she got him, she wanted him to drop instantly, without being able to cause any more damage to Parker or the kids or the other hostages.

It was different from target practice. There she normally visualized the hit and focused on the hole the bullet would leave in the paper. But she blanched at the thought of a bullet busting through Ivan's skull, even if he *was* the enemy. A real person was nothing like the shadow outline at the range.

And what if she missed? There were hostages around him. Bet Parker never thought about missing. He saw what had to be done and did it.

She had to try. He had seconds left at best. Nobody could last longer in his current untenable position.

As the hostages scrambled away from between Parker and Ivan, scared that a stray bullet would find them, Ivan filled the gap by grabbing Katja and holding her in front of him.

Parker couldn't do anything now. But she could. Ivan still hadn't noticed that she'd come down the stairs, and in her direction, his side and head were still unprotected. Katja, however, did look at her, tears streaking her cheeks.

Cold fury steadied Kate as she watched the hard grip Ivan kept on the child's arm, yanking on her when she struggled against him. She took a deep breath, held it so her body wouldn't move, then squeezed the trigger.

She didn't hit her intended target, little wonder. But the bullet did go through Ivan's neck. He dropped his gun and Katja at the same time to clasp both hands to the wound, turning to give Kate a surprised look. A couple of men from among the hostages threw themselves on top of him the next second. Anna, the young woman who'd sat next to her in the gym at the beginning, threw herself on the children to protect them from the bullets that kept coming from the corner. Another hostage finally got hold of Ivan's gun and shot back.

She could only pray that he was a good shot and wouldn't hit Parker.

The sound of boots came from somewhere above her head.

No, no, no. She lunged back up the stairs, taking them two at a time, and locked the door, knowing the simple lock could only hold them for a few seconds.

She clicked the safety on her weapon and shoved it into the waistband of her pants. A handful of wooden boards lay on the shelving that lined the staircase. She grabbed those and wedged them against the door.

She searched desperately for anything else that she could use to strengthen the barricade, knocking tools and a length of rope to the ground, finding an axe that she could think of no use for. Then she accepted that this was the best she could do, and ran back to Parker.

Whoever was in the corner of the basement was still shooting at him. She stuck her head out from the cover of the staircase, then ducked back quickly when the next shot came her way.

"Stay where you are," Parker called out.

She didn't have to be told twice.

At least he was still alive. The same couldn't be said for Ivan. The hostages were using his body for cover. They seemed to have finished the job she had started. His neck looked broken.

Another one of the hostages had the gun now, the tall, young guy whose cooperation she had tried to get unsuccessfully in the gym. He wasn't shooting, however. She supposed he couldn't clearly see the rebel soldier in the corner from where he was and he didn't want to risk hitting Parker. She appreciated the restraint.

Anna was still protecting the children. Everyone was trying to get their ropes off. She wished she could get to them and help, but Parker had asked her to stay, and if she lunged forward she might distract him.

To hell with that. She had to help. She could just warn him that she was going over. She opened her mouth to call out just as he dropped and rolled, found better cover, the giant steel toolbox. He'd left streaks of blood on the cement floor where he touched down. *Shot.* He'd been shot again. Judging from the blood on the ground, this time it was more serious than just a graze. He looked strong and alert, as capable as ever, but at this rate, she was worried how long that could possibly last.

They'd made it this far together. There was no way she would hang back in the stairway and watch him get killed.

The hostages seemed to be able to manage on their own for now. She had to get to Parker and help him, see how bad his latest injury was.

"Coming." Kate bent low and dashed toward him, yelling, "Cover me!" to the hostage who had the gun, hoping like hell that the man spoke English.

He did, and she reached Parker with only a few bullets whizzing by her. Blood pumped through her ears so loudly she could barely hear what he said, but she had no problem interpreting the black thunder on his face.

"I said stay, dammit," he yelled, popped up to fire a few shots over the large steel box then ducked back down again. "Kate, listen to me." He cupped her face with his free hand, forcing her to look at him. His whole body was wound tight, his features hard, his stance promising violence. But not to her. His hand remained gentle. "I'm trying to keep you alive."

"I'm fine."

"You were in a safer position on the stairs. Do you want to die?" His tone reflected his frustration. He let her go and popped up to fire another round.

"Do you?" She grabbed his arm then put her gun on the floor and ripped his shirt-sleeve off, used it to wrap the arm and slow the flow of blood. The bullet had gone clear through the thick cords of muscle.

He kept taking shots the whole time, not at all interested in making her job easier. She did it anyway. He could be stubborn, but so could she.

"Are you okay?" he asked when he dropped down again and looked her over.

She was not okay. Frankly, she thought it was a major miracle that they were still alive. She was hungry and tired and ached just about everywhere. She was pretty close to losing it, more scared than she had ever been in her life. But Parker needed backup. And the hostages were depending on them.

"Good as new," she said.

He gave her a look that said she hadn't fooled him. "It's almost over."

She hoped he was right.

"I can't see him. I'm never going to hit him from here. I have to get closer," he said.

She didn't want him to go. "I'll cover you."

He moved fast, in a zigzag pattern. She shot round after round, aiming well over his head to make sure she didn't hit him by accident. She didn't stop firing until he was safely behind a half wall.

And then he disappeared.

She blinked, trying to bring his outline into focus in the deep shadows. But as hard as she stared, he didn't seem to be there. She hadn't heard any noise, either.

Silence enveloped the basement. The rebel soldier was probably listening for Parker, trying to figure out where he was. The hostages waited for their fate to be decided. They knew their best bet for getting out of here was Parker. Because even if the Tarkmez soldier in the corner got put out of commission, they still had a full rebel team in the building. Kate glanced toward the staircase, surprised that nobody had broken through her makeshift barricade yet. Could be that whoever was coming this way had been waylaid by the Russians. She hoped so. Their plate was kind of full for the time being down here.

A second ticked by, then another. Silence stretched, and as more and more time passed, the tension became nerve-racking.

Maybe Parker had passed out from blood loss. She couldn't accurately judge how much time had passed since he'd gone. It felt like an eternity. Could be he'd reached the rebel and they'd silently knifed each other to death.

Another minute or so passed before the rebel called out, words she didn't understand. Didn't sound like he was giving up, more like taunting.

Okay, that one was still alive. What about Parker?

She wished he, too, would say something, but understood that it would give away his location.

The muted sounds of gunfire came from a couple of floors above them. Sounded like the Russians were well into the building.

The rebel in the corner made a surprised sound, drawing her attention back to him. There was a single gunshot, then some scraping noise. Then complete silence again.

"Parker?" She didn't worry about giving away her location. Everyone already knew where she was.

For a second, no response came, and her heart stopped in midbeat.

The battle seemed to be intensifying upstairs. But her full attention was on Parker as he came out of the shadows. He looked tired and bloody, but he walked tall, his eyes finding her immediately. And what she saw in those eyes took her breath away as effectively as the danger had just moments ago.

She had been crazy to think she could ever walk away from him.

He stopped a foot from her and picked up the TNT belts from the floor, even managed a grin, although she could tell it took some effort. "Let's leave with a bang."

"You know what to do with that?" she asked as a vivid picture of the whole building collapsing on their heads flashed into her mind.

"Does Bugatti make the best cars?" His grin grew wider.

Not only did he know his way around plastic explosives, he looked as though he actually enjoyed playing with them.

He handed her his knife. "Why don't you go check on the hostages? I'll take care of the escape route."

"Okay," she said, and did as he asked.

Half the hostages were already free of

their ropes, having helped each other. She helped the rest.

"Almost over," she told the ambassador's daughters, who were tightly hanging on to each other. "We are leaving here in a minute."

"I want my mommy," the younger one said as new tears welled in her beautiful brown eyes.

"Soon," she lied and ran a soothing hand over her mussed-up hair. "Would you like something to eat?" She emptied her pockets and shirt and every bite of food was snatched up in a second.

Only one of the hostages stayed motionless on the ground. Anna.

Kate moved to her side. "Are you okay?" Then she gasped as she turned her and saw the blood on the woman's chest. A stray bullet had found her as she had shielded the children with her body.

"Parker?" She pressed her hand to the wound, and Anna's eyes fluttered. "We're going to get you out of here," she whispered to the woman.

The girls pressed up against her, one on each side, hanging on to her, watching Anna wide-eyed.

"Keep her still," Parker said, looking over from where he was rigging up the charges.

"Is she going to die?" Katja asked.

"No, honey. She's hurt but she is going to be fine."

The sounds of fighting from above were growing louder. The Alpha troopers were getting closer.

Parker said something in Russian to the hostages. Everyone put on their gas masks, shoving in the last pieces of food first. Kate helped Anna and the girls.

"It feels funny," Elena said, trying to take hers off after a few seconds.

Kate stayed her hands. "Let's pretend it's a game," she said. "Do you know what Halloween is?"

The girls shook their heads.

"Do you ever put on a costume to look like a princess or a pirate or anything like that?"

"A masquerade?" Elena's voice sounded strange through the mask and they giggled.

"Let's pretend it's a masquerade."

"What are we?" Katja asked with caution, not completely buying the story yet.

"Monsters," Kate said, offering the first thing that came to mind. "Undersea monsters."

"Where are your fins?" Elena asked.

She improvised. "We are finless monsters."

"Everything in the sea has fins," said Elena doubtfully.

Kate's mind worked in slow motion, unable to ignore the dying woman in her arms. She couldn't fall apart. She couldn't let the kids see how desperate the situation was. "Not everything." She scrambled for an example, relieved when she found one. "The octopus doesn't."

"You don't look like an ocpopus." Katja touched her hand. "You don't have enough arms. You look like Shrek. Except for the ears."

She glanced around at the others and could see no resemblance to the animated figure, except that the gas masks had a greenish tint. "Do you like Shrek?"

"She loves *Shrek,*" Elena said. "We watched it in Russian and in English, too. Mrs. Miller lets us watch movies in English. She said it helps our pronceation."

Pronunciation, most likely. Kate smiled without correcting her. "Sounds like a smart woman. Your English is very good."

"Where is Mrs. Miller?" the younger one asked.

"She got hurt," Kate said after a moment of hesitation.

"Is she dead?" Elena asked.

"I'm not sure," she told them. She hated lying but the situation was still dangerous. They had to keep their cool. They had to get out of here. It would be better for the children to stay as calm as possible. She couldn't tell them in the middle of utter chaos that their parents *and* their nanny were dead.

"You should be Princess Fiona. You know, when she is an ogre," the younger one said. "Your voice sounds a little like Fiona."

Her gaze sought out Parker, who was now working with a couple of men by the wall. He had a makeshift scale made from a stick, two small boxes and some rope. He was measuring TNT against bags of salt.

Measurements that would be crucial.

She hoped his scale was up to the job.

Next he inspected the walls of the two-hundred-year-old palace. God knew what TNT was going to do to them. Parker knew, she corrected herself. He looked as though he knew exactly what he was doing. He was drilling a hole straight through the wall. Probably to measure the thickness.

"I have to go to the bathroom," Elena said.

"Me, too," her sister chimed in immediately.

"Can you ask that lady?" Kate motioned with her hand toward one of the hostages.

But Katja wouldn't let her go. "I want you to come with me," she begged.

The woman must have understood English, because she came over to put her hand on Anna's wound. But Kate was reluctant to let go, and when she did, she couldn't look away from the blood that covered her hands. And the girls were reaching for her.

She wiped her palm on her black slacks as best she could before Katja and Elena grabbed on to her. Not that she had any idea where to take them. She headed toward an out-of-sight corner of the basement, hoping they would come across an old mop bucket.

But Parker was speaking in Russian again. Then to her. "Get behind cover."

"Can you wait another minute?" she asked the girls, relieved when they nodded.

She followed the rest of the hostages to the half wall Parker had hidden behind earlier. They squatted snugly against each other. Everyone except Parker.

Then he came flying around the wall. "Keep your heads down. She's gonna blow."

Kate tightened her arms around the girls. "Plug your ears."

The explosion that shook the basement the next second knocked them off their feet.

August 12, 03:10

"STAY DOWN," Parker said in Russian then repeated in English for Kate's sake. He straightened to look at his handiwork in the settling dust, and smiled. "Okay. Let's get going."

He strode to the hole first, kicked a few bricks out of the way, checked a couple more overhead to make sure they wouldn't fall on anyone. He looked through the hole. The basement floor in the neighboring building was at least eight feet below them, the space narrow. He looked closer as the dust settled. Maybe it wasn't a basement at all, but some sort of secret passageway that had been walled off. The important thing was that it led out of here.

"Hurry." He helped the first guy over, held him by the arms and lowered his bulk, the man's feet dangling. Then he let go and the man landed with a thud on the floor below. Parker tossed a flashlight after him. "Everything okay?"

"*Da,*" the man responded in his own language.

The next man had an easier time as he had assistance both from above and below. Then came the next and the next, Parker getting a number of handshakes and thank you's.

The children went next, clinging to Kate.

"I'll be coming in a second," she soothed them.

And he after her. He would see her to safety then come back for Piotr. That would have to be dealt with. Soon. Once he had made sure Kate was safe.

He helped a woman down, looking at Anna. Now that the girls had gone ahead, Kate was back at the young woman's side again. Getting Anna down would be difficult. She was unconscious and wouldn't be able to hang on to anything.

Kate caught his gaze. "I think I saw a good chunk of canvas on the shelf by the stairs. We can lower her in that." She ran off for it.

Parker helped another guy in the meantime, then the next woman. It was slow going. She was shaky from nerves and exhaustion. All the hostages were dehydrated and weak from hunger. Whatever little food Kate and he had been able to share hadn't meant much after three days.

The woman slipped several times, and he was about to recommend that she wait and be lowered in the canvas, too, but then she finally made it, teary-eyed from the effort.

Only Anna was left. She was coming to, but was still too weak to move. While he made a rudimentary bandage for her chest to slow the blood loss, he explained to her how they would lower her through the hole.

"You need help up there?" he called up the stairs. The force of the explosion could have knocked over the shelves. Kate was taking too long.

No response came. The short hairs prickled at his nape.

He pulled his gun. "You go. Quick," he told the hostages who were already on the other side. "Stay here," he instructed Anna. "I'm going to come back for you." Then he was off, running for the stairs.

Empty.

His heart about stopped, his lungs too tight to draw in air. He couldn't let anything happen to Kate now. They had a way out. They'd made it this far, against all odds. In minutes they would be free and clear.

But Kate had disappeared, and the basement door was open. He saw the boards on the stairs, figured she had put those up earlier. She'd been under a lot of stress. She hadn't thought to check that the door opened outward. The boards had meant nothing. And the explosion probably had blown the door open. Then Kate went up. And someone who had come to investigate the noise grabbed her.

Parker moved up the stairs with care, watching for any sign of a possible ambush waiting for him at the top. He should have gotten her out of here immediately, no matter the cost. He should have thrown her across his shoulder, should have knocked her out if he'd had to.

If anything happened to her—

He never had any trouble with his focus; his survival depended on it in his line of work. But he was having trouble now, thinking beyond the fact that the bastards had her. It would take them minutes to figure out that she wasn't one of the embassy staff. She didn't speak Russian.

He got to the top, gun ready, moving inch by slow inch when he wanted to fly to her. But he couldn't get killed. To save her, he couldn't afford as much as a single wrong move.

He stepped forward, low. Quick look to the left. Clear. Kicked the door shut so he could look behind it. Nobody there. The hallway was empty in both directions.

For a moment he thought of Anna, waiting for him down below. He wasn't going to forget about her, but for now she had to wait. He hoped her weakness came more from lack of food and water than from her wound. She wasn't bleeding that badly. Then again, she could be bleeding internally. He had promised that he'd be back for her. And he would. But he had to get Kate before it was too late.

The sounds of combat filled his ears. He listened for Kate's voice. Any words of arguing, crying or screaming. He heard nothing.

Out-and-out war was being fought on the floors above him. Machine-gun fire, small explosions. Smoke lingered in the air. Judging from the sounds, the battle was at a fever pitch, neither side holding anything back.

Anger and desperation gave him new strength, until he could barely recall his own injuries. He pushed forward with grim determination.

The building was a death trap.

And he had lost Kate.

Chapter Eleven

August 12, 03:30

"Don't. Please." She fought against the beefy man who was dragging her along, keeping his gun firmly pressed against her temple. Piotr. She recognized him from earlier when he'd fought with Parker in the kitchen.

The man with the chemical-agent capsules. The man who had nothing to lose. That put her at a serious disadvantage when it came to negotiating with him. He probably figured that since he had succeeded in avenging his father's death, he could die happily now, whatever happened. Great.

"Can we just stop and talk?" She tried anyway. She'd come too far to give up now.

He didn't bother to respond. He held his gun in his left hand. His right wrist, which Parker had shot, was bandaged with a piece of blood-soaked cloth. Didn't seem to slow him down much.

He had come out of nowhere, from behind her as she had tried to free the canvas for Anna from all the junk on one of the shelves. The explosion had rattled the door enough to shake off the boards. He must have had the lock already opened by the time she got up there. He'd been lurking outside, waiting.

She could have screamed for Parker, but she didn't want to draw Piotr's attention to the people who were escaping through the basement. She wanted to keep him away from the rest of the hostages, from Anna and the kids. So she went with him, struggling only to slow him down as much as possible.

Parker would come for her. She knew it in her heart. In the past she'd been angry at him for never being there for her, for always being away when she needed him. But in the last couple of days she'd gotten to know him better than she ever had before. And she realized that when she'd truly needed him, he'd always been there.

Maybe he hadn't come along to pick out china patterns, but he had been there in the Florida night when those thugs accosted her. There were times a woman *thought* she needed her man. Then there were times when she *truly* needed him. So he'd never gone shopping with her. But the truth was, while she'd been out shopping, he'd been out saving lives, lives of people like Anna and the kids below. She wished she'd known that.

"Move it." Piotr shoved her roughly.

Parker will come. She fixed the thought firmly in her mind. She believed in him and trusted him one hundred percent. She'd thought him undependable before, too focused on his reporting career to care about others. She'd been wrong. She wanted to live long enough to tell him that.

But living even a few more minutes seemed less than likely.

She no longer had her gun, was grateful that at least her mask hadn't been ripped away from her face. Her captor wore his own. Smoke rolled through the hallway he dragged her along. Smoke and maybe something else. Bodies lined the floor, most of them rebels, only two Russian elite-force soldiers so far that she could see.

She looked for signs of what had killed the men. Plenty of bullet holes in the bodies. Which didn't mean that there wasn't gas in the air.

He dragged her into the back staircase that was deserted at the moment. They went up.

"Please let me go. I have nothing to do with this. I'm an American." She figured at this stage she had nothing to lose by revealing that. Things were already as bad as they could get.

"I know all about Americans." The man then picked up speed as fresh gunfire sounded from above.

"Listen to me. I'm the American Consul. I can be your ticket out of here." She gasped for air. He was going way too fast, not letting her catch her breath. "We can walk right out of here, the two of us. Nobody will hurt you as long as you have me."

They exited the staircase and rushed down the long corridor ahead, took several turns. The man shoved her into some nicely furnished parlor that looked as though it had seen its share of fighting tonight. Chairs and antique tables lay broken on the expensive carpet, bullet holes pocked in the walls. The lights were off, but she could see clearly since floodlights lit the front of the building from the outside and the large French doors that lined one wall let plenty of light into the room.

They'd come up two flights of stairs and she had no idea of her location otherwise.

"We have to go back down. We have to get out of the building. We can go out the front. The media is there. Nobody will shoot you with me in front of you."

Movement caught her eye on the other side of the French doors. Her breath caught. Parker? The Russians?

It meant the difference between life and death. She didn't dare look that way, afraid that if it was Parker, she'd give him away. But whoever it was didn't come in. She waited, her captor talking into his cell phone, barking questions and instructions she didn't understand.

Come on, Parker. Come on.

She moved so he would have a clear shot if that was what he was waiting for, pulling away from Piotr as much as he allowed her. She waited for the shot. Nothing happened.

Her captor put away his phone and focused on her. She had to keep him occupied.

"I know the freedom of your people is important to you. If you die here today, you won't be able to fight for it again. It's useless to die now. This battle is lost. But if you stay alive, you can help your people win the war. I can help you get out of here safely."

She was handling the situation. Managing

the problem. She managed everything. That was who she was, what she did. Except she'd never been able to manage Parker, and she realized only now, too late, that a man like Parker could never be managed. Should never be managed.

Piotr grabbed for her with his left hand as quick as a snake and ripped her gas mask off, tossing it aside.

"I'm fighting for no people. I'm fighting for me," he said. "I already got what I came here for."

And she remembered now Parker telling her that he wasn't even Tarkmezi. He was Russian, with his own agenda—an agenda that had already been accomplished. Which didn't leave her with much leverage.

She gasped the smoky air. Her lungs contracted as if they were ready to collapse. Oh God, there *was* gas in the air.

She clawed at her throat, scared out of her mind now, her eyes filling with tears. But a few minutes passed and she was still alive, and she realized her reaction was caused by the smoke and her own panic. She fought to slow her breathing and get a lungful of air.

"Who are you?" Piotr watched her dispassionately with eyes that looked small and watery blue through the glass of his mask.

"I'm a Consul of the United States of America. We have to help each other." She coughed.

"What are you doing here?" he asked, then, "Doesn't matter." He had relaxed his gun for a few moments, but now he pressed it hard against her head again.

She gasped for breath, expecting it to be her last, casting a desperate glance to the French door. And caught sight of movement again, and this time, she could see what it was. She could have cried with despair.

Out there, in the night breeze, fluttered the white, blue and red cloth of the Russian flag. That was the movement she had mistaken for Parker.

They were at the front balcony of the building, the place the rebels had used to throw out bodies of hostages to make a point in front of the press who camped outside.

And she was the last hostage they had. Parker was even now saving the others through the basement.

Her limbs froze. She understood with terrifying clarity what Piotr's plan was.

Parker was coming for her. She had no

doubt of that. But he had no way of knowing where she was. And there was fighting all over the building. He might be held back for a while yet.

Time was something she no longer had.

What they said about your life flashing through your mind before you die was true. Scenes of her and Parker flickered across the TV screen of her brain—the good times and the bad. She wanted to tell him that she was sorry that she had walked away without giving him a second chance. God, she wanted to tell him so much, wanted to feel his arms around her one last time.

But the cold metal of the barrel pressed against her temple as Piotr shoved her toward the French doors that led to the balcony.

"This is for that interfering bastard friend of yours," he said.

HE KNEW exactly where they would take her. And if he was right, she didn't have much time.

Parker burst into the staircase.

Unfortunately, two rebels crashed through the door on the level above him at the same time. He shot without hesitation, got one of them, but the other flattened himself in the doorway. Parker crept upward, glad that whatever negligible noise he made was swallowed by the sounds of battle above.

When he came to the turn in the stairs where he presented a clear target, he blanketed the enemy position with fire. No answering shots came. He found out why when he reached the top of the stairs. The second guy was dead, too.

He stepped over the bodies, ran up one more flight and pushed the door open slowly. Thin smoke settled like fog in the hallway. He heard plenty of fighting, but saw none of it at the moment and was keen to take advantage of that.

Something heavy crashed to the floor above him. Much heavier than a body. Furniture? He ran toward the front of the building.

He found fighting as soon as he turned the corner. A black-clad Alpha trooper was holding off two rebels. He had nothing against the Alphas; they were a fine special-forces team. But right now, the guy was standing between him and Kate, holding him back, and that he could not allow. The rebels had noticed Parker and were shooting at him already. He shot back, clearing the way before him.

The guy in black didn't give himself easily. His skill level was several notches higher than the rebels' and his bulletproof vest was a good one, with a ceramic insert that stood up to rifle fire as well as handguns. But there were places it didn't cover. And Parker was an excellent shot. The man went down.

He picked up the guy's semiautomatic rifle and checked it for ammunition. Half a magazine. He shoved his handgun, which was close to empty, into the back of his waistband then broke into a run.

He found the right hallway, but didn't know which was the right room.

An explosion came from somewhere above, toward the back of the building. The rear balcony? Gunfire intensified. A full-on attack. Did that mean the hostages had made it out so the Alpha troops knew they no longer had to worry about them?

He opened one door after the other. Some rooms stood untouched, while others showed signs of combat: smashed furniture and bullet holes in the walls and flooring. Then he got to the right one, could hear Kate's voice through the closed door. He couldn't make out the words, but the fear and desperation came through. He backed up a step and kicked the door in.

"Parker!"

Two things claimed his immediate attention: Piotr, who held a gun to Kate's head and was just about to take her out to the balcony, and the Vymple team guy, who entered the room through another entrance at the same time as Parker had.

Vymple was the Russian special forces. The Colonel had told him they were here along with the Alpha troops, but this was the first guy he'd seen.

Parker's gun was trained on Piotr. Piotr kept his on Kate. The newcomer put Parker in the crosshairs. A three-way standoff. And two out of the three men in the room probably didn't care much who lived and who died.

Kate coughed.

The smoke was getting thicker. She was the only one who didn't have a mask.

Piotr surprised them all by tossing Kate aside in a sudden movement, practically slamming her into the floor, and shooting at the Russian with a fierce cry, hitting his target with the first shot, right through the left eye glass.

The next second his gun was on Parker. Kate was now between him and Piotr so he had to be careful. She was coughing again, trying to come to her feet, but went down again.

Was she hurt? He could see no blood. Dammit. What was in the air? He needed to know how much danger she was in.

"I don't know how my friends missed you, but I'm not going to make the same mistake, McCall."

"Since when do you have Tarkmez friends?"

"Since they promised to give me what I want."

"Victor?"

"My only regret is that it was over so fast. I would have preferred to savor it."

"So he's dead. You have what you wanted."

"What I want is another forty years, but I'm not likely to get it. The doctors give me six months at the most. But you, you have nine lives. I sent four of my best men after you when I realized you followed me to Paris. You're supposed to be three days dead and six feet under. And yet here you are."

Parker watched the man, wondered what his illness might be—he didn't look weakened yet, whatever it was—realized that his plan was probably to go out in a blaze of glory instead of a hospital bed. Piotr was here on a suicide mission.

He wasn't surprised that Piotr had sent the men after him. He had suspected as much. Piotr seemed to be at the center of a lot of things.

"You're all right, you know," the man was saying now. "Almost as good as I am. Just have bad judgment. Picked the wrong side."

"How about we let her go?" Parker nodded toward Kate without taking his eyes off Piotr. "Then we'll see who is better. Just you and me. A man deserves a little fun before dying."

Piotr seemed to consider the offer for a moment, but then shook his head.

Parker tossed his rifle as if giving up, then pulled his handgun from the back of his waistband. The bullet hit Piotr in the throat.

He was beside Kate before the man even hit the ground, ripping Piotr's mask off and securing it on her face. "Are you okay?" He kept his weapon on Piotr to be on the safe side.

"I think so."

But she wouldn't have been that way for long, a fact that became obvious when Piotr began to twitch on the floor, his eyes going wide, drool running out of his mouth. He wouldn't have done that from the shot. Somebody had just released nerve gas in the air.

"Let's go." He pulled Kate up and grabbed her by the arm, glanced back when she hobbled.

"What's wrong with your leg?"

"I don't know. It doesn't seem to hold me up," she said just as another explosion shook the building. "I can limp along."

"Not fast enough."

He picked her up in his arms, looking for blood again and still not finding any. So she hadn't been hit by a stray bullet. She must have torn a tendon or dislocated her ankle. No time to stop and look at it.

The smoke in the hallway was blacker and thicker than just minutes ago. He saw open flames to his right so he turned left.

"Hang on tight." He could only support her with one arm; the other he needed to hold his weapon.

The conditions in the building were deteriorating fast. They needed to take the shortest way out. One floor down and through the main lobby.

His left arm was still bleeding, not terribly

so, but he had lost enough blood by now to make him feel weaker. Add to that the lack of food and sleep and he knew he wasn't in top shape. It would come down to seconds and to his last ounce of strength. He pushed forward with everything he had.

One rebel was running up the main staircase. His first shot at Parker went wide. The second didn't go anywhere. He was out of bullets. He was a young guy, without a mask, the fear on his face distorting his features.

Parker lowered his weapon and ran by him on his way down the wide stairs.

Then they were in the main lobby where four rebel soldiers held the main entrance, barricaded with desks and chairs and whatever furniture they had been able to find. One of them was wearing a TNT belt.

Their attention was focused outward so Parker had a split-second chance to step behind the row of metal detectors to the side. The Russian embassy had a pretty decent system to scan entering visitors.

Kate must have been thinking the same because she asked, "How do you think the rebels got in here in the first place?"

"Could be they had inside help." Ivan came to mind. Could be he was Piotr's connection. "I figure Piotr gave the rebels Ivan and a way in, and in exchange the rebels brought him along, giving him a chance to take out Victor, who was pretty much guaranteed to be here."

Piotr was the only Russian among the attackers, a man with connections everywhere. Ivan was also Russian. Could be he hadn't even fully known what he was doing when he'd compromised embassy security for Piotr. They'd had a deal. That was why he was the only embassy guard the rebels had left alive.

"I am sorry about before. When I left—" Kate said out of the blue as he slipped her to the ground.

He'd been focused on the rebels so her words caught him by surprise. His heart thumped. He wished they didn't have to have the masks on so he could see her eyes.

"I'm sorry, too." The words broke free from deep in his chest.

He'd been a fool. And why in hell was he holding back still?

"I was crazy to let you go," he said the words out loud. Well, more like in a whisper, although there was enough fighting going on in the building to cover the sound of his voice. But if ever there was a time to lay all his cards on the table, this was it.

Possibly their last chance, although he preferred not to dwell on that.

She nodded slowly. "If we don't make it—"

He pulled her into his arms to silence her, although the same thought lay heavily on his mind. To hell with that. They *were* going to make it. They had to. He was not going to lose her again. He'd be damned if he died just when he finally got her back. So the deal was, both of them were going to make it. He would accept no other outcome.

"I want to have dinner with you tomorrow night," he said, and wished he could kiss her, but they couldn't afford to take their masks off even for a second. So instead, he caressed what little of her face was uncovered.

Then he turned to fight. But she held him back.

"Give me one of the guns."

He hesitated only a split second before handing her the Russian-made Makarov he'd taken off Piotr.

They opened fire simultaneously. His first shot hit its target, hers missed by inches. The remaining three rebels scattered as they shot back, running for cover.

He aimed for the one with the explosives and brought him down. The man fell behind a makeshift barricade, so Parker couldn't tell whether he was injured or dead. He focused on the other two. Kate did, too, and finished one of them off. The remaining guy, however, managed to give them a fair amount of trouble.

He was a good shot, the best of the bunch, and the quickest. Parker swore as a bullet grazed his knee. He couldn't let his legs get injured. He had to carry Kate out of here.

He waited and took his time, held back until he saw a flash of movement through the cracks in the piled-up furniture. He took the shot. There was no responding hail of bullets.

"We'd better—" Kate was moving forward already, limping heavily, but he held out a hand to stop her.

He went first, slow and cautious, rifle aimed at the spot where he had fired his last shot. No movement. He walked toward the side instead of in a straight line. In another two steps, he could see the motionless body on the floor.

"Okay." He went back to Kate and picked her up, but still kept his weapon handy. He held her tight. "You cover me from the back."

She looked over his shoulder and brought up the Makarov. "You bet."

He made his way through the barricade, kicking chairs aside, stepping over a lifeless body. Then he was at the outer door.

Wow. He was seeing two. Double vision. Not a good sign. The blood he was losing through his latest injury was pushing his already damaged body over the edge.

Just a little more.

"We can't go out armed." He dropped his rifle, hating being unarmed.

Kate's Makarov clattered to the marble behind him. He opened the door that, thank God, was unlocked. The rebels probably hadn't been able to figure out the electronic lock mechanism or override the program's password.

He was blinded by the floodlights that immediately hit him. Pain pulsed in his arm and leg, his vision growing hazier, even though there was no smoke out here. But he could make out a police cordon and more barricades—triangular cement boulders with dozens of armed men behind them. He staggered that way, holding on tightly to Kate.

Then an explosion shook the ground and a wave of fire shot out from the door behind him to claim them.

THAT WAS the picture that made the front page of *Le Figaro* the next day, as well as the front page of most major newspapers around the world. Parker lurching forward in the moment of explosion, Kate in his arms, the flames obscuring most of the building behind them.

"A rescue-team member saves one of the hostages," the caption said in dozens of languages. Neither their names nor nationality were mentioned. The gas masks had kept their faces covered.

Epilogue

As it turned out, they didn't have dinner the next night, or the night after that. Parker was immediately recalled to the U.S. for treatment and debriefing. Although the Colonel had been able to pull enough strings to keep his identity secret, the Russians were more than interested in the hero the surviving hostages were talking about. Not to the press, though. The survivors said little to the army of reporters. A gag order had been issued regarding the incident.

The official story was that the rescue had been carried out by internal embassy security.

Good enough for him, Parker thought as he drove down the Avenue de la Bourdonnais two weeks later, too nervous to enjoy the early-twentieth-century architecture of the upscale seventh arrondissement. It had taken him this long to get back into Paris. The Colonel had refused to let him go until his wounds healed.

The first gunshot, that little scrape, had given him the most trouble. The wound itself hadn't been bad, but since it had gone untreated for a while, he'd managed to develop a nasty infection. All better now, save for the slight limp he still had from the third shot, which he did his best to hide.

He found the building he was looking for, a gorgeous villa in the nicest section of the avenue. He parked right in front of the house, allowed to do so by the security guard. He was expected.

His heart beat an expectant rhythm as he stepped out of his rental Renault Mégane convertible, or cabriolet, as they called it around here. Not a bad car. Might have to consider one for his collection. He grabbed the ridiculously large bouquet of pink roses from the passenger seat.

He ran up the walkway, nodded back to the security guard who opened the door for him. The hallway reflected Kate's taste, classy but with a swirl of heat. The antique furniture was French to match the historical building, the art modern and full of fire. He recognized a few pieces from the condo they had shared together: the four-foot-tall, red Murano glass vase, prints of the bold paintings of Raoul Dufy that Kate collected.

Then everything else disappeared as he looked up and spotted her at the top of the wide curving staircase.

"Hi." She gave a shy smile, stealing his breath.

She wore shimmering black silk that hugged her body, her hair swept up to leave her graceful neck free. She wore the earrings he had long ago given her.

He desperately wanted that to mean something.

She had said she regretted the past. Said it when she'd thought they'd both be dead the next second. He wasn't sure how much stock he could put in that, although he wanted it to be true.

"Come on up," she said with a smile. "We'll be having dinner on the balcony."

He took the steps two at a time, feeling embarrassingly eager. Then they were on the same level, her jewel eyes shining. At him. He handed her the roses, still unable to say a word.

"Thank you."

"Sorry I couldn't come earlier." He leaned

forward, not sure what to do. In the end, he brushed his lips over hers.

She didn't pull back. "How is your arm? How is your leg?"

Did she notice his limp? "Better. Great." He swept in for another kiss. "You taste like strawberries," he said.

She smiled. "I just tested our dessert."

"You ate my dessert?" He tried to sound outraged, but couldn't pull it off.

"A tiny taste. Quality control."

"A taste for a taste." He lowered his head again and this time kissed her as though he meant it.

She opened to him, letting him take what he wanted, taking what she needed in return. She gave him back all that he had thought he'd lost.

"How is your ankle?" he asked a while later.

"I tore a ligament when I fell. It'll heal. Anna has been released from the hospital."

He knew. The Colonel had told him when he inquired about the hostages. Turned out Anna was the inside man, well, woman in this case, for the French. Every embassy in every country has inside men-slash-women, sometimes several: admin staff hired in the host country to observe and report to their own government on the comings and goings at the embassy.

"She called me to see if I could tell her how to reach you. She wanted to thank you for going back in for her."

"No thanks are necessary." He didn't remember much of that part of the night. He'd been half unconscious from pain. He'd left Kate with the French police at the ambulance, then had charged back in through the fire with a commando team to show them where he'd left the injured young woman.

To his surprise, they'd found Ivan, too, still alive, and brought out both of them. The hostages had broken his neck, but he would survive—a paraplegic. He had given a full confession already, confirming Parker's suspicions about his connection to Piotr.

A Tarkmezi warlord had apparently put out word that he needed someone with a connection at the Russian embassy in Paris. Piotr, who needed the warlord's favor on some gun deal, made a point of finding a "friend" via blackmail. Then, when he realized what the warlord needed the connection for, he got himself on the team, knowing that it would allow him to meet the leader of Russia's antiterrorist unit—the man who'd killed his father. Meet him and take him out. A tangled mess of private agendas.

"I heard the girls are back in Russia," he said.

Kate smiled. "With their aunt. They have a brand-new baby in the family. Katja is very excited not to be the smallest. I called them."

He smiled. She was the type of person who would. She'd make sure the kids were happy and if not, she'd do something about it.

He lifted her into his arms, not because she seemed to still favor the bad ankle, but because he wanted to hold her as close as possible. "Which way?"

"Second door on the right."

He was there in seconds, making his way in. "This doesn't look like the balcony." He grinned toward the sprawling bed in the middle of the room.

"Oh dear, did I get turned around again?" she asked, all innocence.

He felt his blood run a little faster. He walked with her to the bed to lay her on the silk sheets. He wanted her now, fast and hard, but he wanted even more to do everything right this time. There were still things he wanted to clear up between them.

"Before we— I want to come clean about

one more thing. I've said before that my uncle and aunt had raised me because my parents were gone. That's not completely true. My mother is still alive somewhere."

He drew a deep breath. He had never told this to anyone. He expected the Colonel knew, that it was in some background check in his file, but the Colonel wasn't the type of man to bring something like this up.

"My mother was a showgirl in Atlantic City, ran by the name of Ruby Russel back then. My father was a cabby, stupid in love with her. She'd leave us from time to time for another guy, always came back in a week or two." He blocked the emotions that came with the memories. "Then, when I was about eight, she left for good. Left for Vegas. About six months later, my father was late coming home. He was always late, no big deal. Sometimes he went to sit at the end of the pier near our apartment and drink a beer, staring at the water.

"I went looking for him. He was there." He could still clearly see him outlined against the moonlight over the ocean. "I yelled to him, but he couldn't hear me over the waves. I was at the end of the pier when he pulled a gun." One he had kept for protection. "By the time I got there, I couldn't see anything but his blood frothing on top of the water."

"Parker." She reached for him, held him. She was crying.

He didn't want her to cry for him. "I told you because— Back when we were— It scared me how much I needed you. I couldn't forget what needing my mother did to my old man."

"Needing other people doesn't have to be bad."

"I know that now. There were other things, too. My life is— You're all light. I thought that the darkness I worked in would somehow suck you in, like what happened with Jake's wife, Elaine. But I'm not going to let that happen, you know?"

He needed her. He needed her the way a dark room needed a candle. He was at a loss as to how to explain what he felt. He held her tightly and looked up, out the oversized, curved window that opened to the sky. "Even the night sky has its moon and stars."

"Is that your way of saying that dark and light could work together?" She gave him a tremulous smile.

"Yeah. The whole yin-yang thing and all."

"I missed you," she said, her clear, luminous gaze holding his.

"I missed you, too." He lay beside her and kissed her again. "But this goes beyond missing. It's not a quick trip to the past, Kate. This is what I want and I want it forever."

"I guess this means you won't be satisfied with a one-night stand?" A mischievous grin played on her full lips, sending his blood racing through his veins.

"Be my wife."

That had the power to make her go all serious.

"It didn't work before…."

"I'm going to make it work this time. I promise."

She didn't say anything.

And he felt nervous all of a sudden. "I'm going to ask for domestic assignments. I'll take on some training at the home base so I can be with you more."

Still no word from her, the look on her face unreadable.

"I want us to get a house like you wanted before. Big yard, dog, cats, canaries, whatever you want," he said. "I want kids. I—"

She put a finger over his lips to stop him, and finally smiled, wide and bright. "I'm okay with what you do. Really. And— Okay, okay. Yes! To everything. It was yes from the beginning. I just didn't want you to know how pitifully in love with you I am." Her face softened with emotion.

"You are?" His heart expanded. "I love you, too." Never stopped, never will.

"Is there a reason why we're still dressed?" she asked.

He was the type of guy who always rose to the challenge. He had them both naked in record time. Her soft skin felt incredible against his. He turned her on her back and came up on his elbow next to her, drew a hand downward, starting at the hollow of her neck.

"I could look at you for a week straight and it wouldn't be enough." He wanted to soak up this moment, the two of them together, safe, in love.

"We just made up. Are you telling me that you're going to disappoint me already? Parker McCall, you'd better do more than look."

He grinned and dipped his head to kiss the nearest nipple, drinking in her sigh of pleasure.

Her body was perfection, but that was the least of the attraction. She was his heart, his soul. He was never going to lose her again.

He caressed her flat abdomen, drawing his fingers to her hip bones and lower. He wanted to get lost inside her, but was holding back, equally needing to savor this moment. He kissed his way down her body and up her inner thigh, relishing the soft trembling of her muscles.

He tasted her, devoured her, needing to make her his, wanting to delete the memory of the time they had spent apart.

And when she arched her back and cried out his name, he finally pushed deep inside her. And her body welcomed him home.

Much later, when he had made love to her every way possible, they lay replete in each other's arms, steeped in pleasure.

"So when does your next mission start?" she asked, even her voice sounding satiated.

"Immediately."

"Oh." She snuggled closer, as if reluctant to let him go.

He liked that.

He gathered her tight into his arms. "My main mission from now on will be to love you senseless and never let you go. We are going to make this work. How fast do you think we could be married?"

She lifted her head to look at him and

smiled. "I'd bet pretty fast. We are in the city of love," she said and pressed her lips to his.

He loved Paris.

* * * * *

Look for LAST WOLF WATCHING
by Rhyannon Byrd—
the exciting conclusion
in the BLOODRUNNERS miniseries
from Silhouette Nocturne.

Follow Michaela and Brody on their fierce
journey to find the truth and face the
demons from the past, as they reach the
heart of the battle between
the Runners and the rogues.

Here is a sneak preview of book three,
LAST WOLF WATCHING.

Michaela squinted, struggling to see through the impenetrable darkness. Everyone looked toward the Elders, but she knew Brody Carter still watched her. Michaela could feel the power of his gaze. Its heat. Its strength. And something that felt strangely like anger, though he had no reason to have any emotion toward her. Strangers from different worlds, brought together beneath the heavy silver moon on a night made for hell itself. That was their only connection.

The second she finished that thought, she knew it was a lie. But she couldn't deal with

it now. Not tonight. Not when her whole
world balanced on the edge of destruction.

Willing her backbone to keep her upright,
Michaela Doucet focused on the towering
blaze of a roaring bonfire that rose from the
far side of the clearing, its orange flames
burning with maniacal zeal against the inky
black curtain of the night. Many of the
Lycans had already shifted into their preter-
natural shapes, their fur-covered bodies
standing like monstrous shadows at the edges
of the forest as they waited with restless ex-
pectancy for her brother.

Her nineteen-year-old brother, Max, had
been attacked by a rogue werewolf—a Lycan
who preyed upon humans for food. Max had
been bitten in the attack, which meant he was
no longer human, but a breed of creature that
existed between the two worlds of man and
beast, much like the Bloodrunners themselves.

The Elders parted, and two hulking shapes
emerged from the trees. In their wolf forms,
the Lycans stood over seven feet tall, their
legs bent at an odd angle as they stalked
forward. They each held a thick chain that
had been wound around their inside wrists,
the twin lengths leading back into the
shadows. The Lycans had taken no more than

a few steps when they jerked on the chains, and her brother appeared.

Bound like an animal.

Biting at her trembling lower lip, she glanced left, then right, surprised to see that others had joined her. Now the Bloodrunners and their family and friends stood as a united force against the Silvercrest pack, which had yet to accept the fact that something sinister was eating away at its foundation—something that would rip down the protective walls that separated their world from the humans'. It occurred to Michaela that loyalties were being announced tonight—a separation made between those who would stand with the Runners in their fight against the rogues and those who blindly supported the pack's refusal to face reality. But all she could focus on was her brother. Max looked so hurt…so terrified.

"Leave him alone," she screamed, her soft-soled, black satin slip-ons struggling for purchase in the damp earth as she rushed toward Max, only to find herself lifted off the ground when a hard, heavily muscled arm clamped around her waist from behind, pulling her clear off her feet. "Damn it, let me down!" she snarled, unable to take her eyes off her brother as the golden-eyed Lycan kicked him.

Mindless with heartache and rage, Michaela clawed at the arm holding her, kicking her heels against whatever part of her captor's legs she could reach. "Stop it," a deep, husky voice grunted in her ear. "You're not helping him by losing it. I give you my word he'll survive the ceremony, but you have to keep it together."

"Nooooo!" she screamed, too hysterical to listen to reason. "You're monsters! All of you! Look what you've done to him! How dare you! *How dare you!*"

The arm tightened with a powerful flex of muscle, cinching her waist. Her breath sucked in on a sharp, wailing gasp.

"Shut up before you get both yourself and your brother killed. I will *not* let that happen. Do you understand me?" her captor growled, shaking her so hard that her teeth clicked together. "Do you understand me, Doucet?"

"Damn it," she cried, stricken as she watched one of the guards grab Max by his hair. Around them Lycans huffed and growled as they watched the spectacle, while others outright howled for the show to begin.

"That's enough!" the voice seethed in her

ear. "They'll tear you apart before you even reach him, and I'll be damned if I'm going to stand here and watch you die."

Suddenly, through the haze of fear and agony and outrage in her mind, she finally recognized who'd caught her. *Brody*.

He held her in his arms, her body locked against his powerful form, her back to the burning heat of his chest. A low, keening sound of anguish tore through her, and her head dropped forward as hoarse sobs of pain ripped from her throat. "Let me go. I have to help him. *Please*," she begged brokenly, knowing only that she needed to get to Max. "Let me go, Brody."

He muttered something against her hair, his breath warm against her scalp, and Michaela could have sworn it was a single word…. But she must have heard wrong. She was too upset. Too furious. Too terrified. She must be out of her mind.

Because it sounded as if he'd quietly snarled the word *never*.

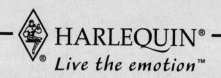

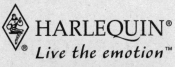

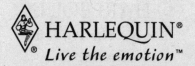

HARLEQUIN®

SuperRomance®

...there's more to the story!

Superromance.
A *big* satisfying read about unforgettable
characters. Each month we offer *six* very different
stories that range from family drama to adventure
and mystery, from highly emotional stories to
romantic comedies—and much more! Stories
about people you'll believe in and care about.
Stories too compelling to put down....

Our authors are among today's *best* romance
writers. You'll find familiar names and talented
newcomers. Many of them are award winners—
and you'll see why!

If you want the biggest and best
in romance fiction, you'll get it
from Superromance!

Exciting, Emotional, Unexpected...

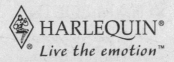

HARLEQUIN®
Live the emotion™

HARLEQUIN®
Presents

The world's bestselling romance series...
The series that brings you your favorite authors,
month after month:

Helen Bianchin...Emma Darcy
Lynne Graham...Penny Jordan
Miranda Lee...Sandra Marton
Anne Mather...Carole Mortimer
Susan Napier...Michelle Reid

and many more uniquely talented authors!

Wealthy, powerful, gorgeous men...
Women who have feelings just like your own...
The stories you love, set in exotic, glamorous locations...

HARLEQUIN®
Presents

Seduction and Passion Guaranteed!

www.eHarlequin.com

HPDIR104